I0779803

WET DREAMS ON LOCKDOWN

The Unit Manager

NAI

URBAN AINT DEAD

URBAN AINT DEAD PRESENTS

Wet Dreams On Lockdown:
The Unit Manager

By Nai

URBAN AINT DEAD
P.O Box 448
Maybrook, NY 12543

No part of this book may be reproduced or transmitted in any form by any means, electronic or mechanical, including photocopying, recording, or by any information storage system, without written permission from the publisher.

Copyright © 2024 By Nai

All rights reserved. Published by URBAN AINT DEAD Publications.

Cover Design: P. Wise / The Wise Services

URBAN AINT DEAD and coinciding logo(s) are registered properties.

No patent liability is assumed with respect to the use of information contained herein. Although every precaution has been taken in the preparation of this book, the publisher and the author assume no responsibility for errors or omissions. Neither is any liability assumed for damages resulting from the use of the information contained herein. This is a work of fiction. Names, characters, places, and incidents are either the product of the author's imagination or are used fictitiously. Any

resemblance to actual events, locales, or persons living or dead is entirely coincidental.

Contact Author on FB: Authoressnai / IG: @authoressnai / TikTok: @authoressnai / Website: hoodloverssociety.com / Email: hoodloverssociety@gmail.com

Contact Publisher at www.urbanaintdead.com

Email: urbanaintdead@gmail.com

CONTENTS

SOUNDTRACKS

Scan the QR Code below to listen to the Soundtracks/Singles
of some of your favorite U.A.D titles:

Don't have Spotify or Apple Music?
No Sweat!
Visit your choice streaming platform and search URBAN
AINT DEAD.

Currently on lock serving a bid?
JPay, iHeartRadio, WHATEVER!
We got you covered.

Simply log into your facility's kiosk or tablet, go to music and search URBAN AINT DEAD.

URBAN AINT DEAD

Like & Follow us on social media:

FB - URBAN AINT DEAD

IG: @urbanaintdead

Tik Tok - @urbanaintdead

SUBMISSIONS

Submit the first three chapters of your completed manuscript to urbanaintdead@gmail.com, subject line: Your book's title. The manuscript must be in a .doc file and sent as an attachment. The document should be in Times New Roman, double-spaced, and in size 12 font. Also, provide your synopsis and full contact information. If sending multiple submissions, they must each be in a separate email. Have a story but no way to submit it electronically? You can still submit to URBAN AINT DEAD. Send in the first three chapters, written or typed, of your completed manuscript to:

URBAN AINT DEAD

P.O Box 448

Maybrook, NY 12543

DO NOT send original manuscript. Must be a duplicate.
Provide your synopsis and a cover letter containing your full contact information.
Thanks for considering URBAN AINT DEAD.

DISCLAIMER

WARNING: I am not responsible for any babies that may be conceived after reading this book. That said, if you must act out your sexual desires after reading and a baby is conceived because of said desires, please contact me directly for the proper spelling of my name. Now, let's get to the fun, shall we.

Chapter 1

CAMILLE

I moaned and panted, thrashing my face from side to side as my lover took complete control of my body with the flick of his tongue. He'd swiped it up and down my slit, stopping at my clit, giving it a light suck, before inserting two fingers inside my love cave. I was so wet and couldn't recall a time I'd experienced this kind of ecstasy. My eyelids became heavy, making it hard to keep my eyes open as and my clit swelled twice its size, and my orgasm grew.

"Mmmhmm, gimmie that shit, baby," he nastily encouraged, adding more pressure, eagerly anticipating the juices

that were sure to pour out of me, and onto his awaiting tongue.

His encouragement was music to my ears as I lifted my right breast and used my long tongue to graze my nipple. "Ooouu, shit, you gon' make me cum," I announced, breathless, grinding my fat pussy in his mouth. He responded by lifting my waist off the bed and sliding his finger into my ass. "Oh, my godddd, what are you doing to me?!" My eyes rolled in the back of my head as my legs shook. "Ooouu, I'm cummin'!!!" The floodgates opened and I squirted, wetting his face up.

"Good girl, Mama." He gave my pussy a light slap before placing me flat on the bed again. Kissing my inner thighs, he made a trail up my body, stopping at my mouth.

Using his tongue to part my full lips, we engaged in the most passionate French kiss. The feeling of him running his dick up and down my slit was heavenly. I fought the urge to guide him into me but remembering his demand to let him have his way with me, I waited anxiously for what was to come. As he slid into me inch by inch, my mouth fell agape, speaking the only audible words that came to mind. "I love you."

"I love you, too," I heard back, and my eyes popped open. Turning my head, I found my boyfriend of a year staring back at me with a goofy smile plastered on his face. "I was tearing that pussy up in yo dream, wasn't I?" Omar thrust his hips upward, playfully humping the air.

"Huh?" I questioned, dumbfounded, with a hint of disappointment laced in my tone that couldn't be missed.

"In yo' dream, bae. You've been moaning and shit for the past eight minutes. I was tempted to put this dick on you, but a nigga just got in from working a double and I know I wouldn't have lasted long." He chuckled like there was a comical line in his statement.

I didn't find his truth funny at all. Not one to crush my man's ego, I gave him a lazy smile and pecked his lips. "Yeah, you were doin' yo shit, bae. I gotta go shower."

Standing up, I felt the wetness from my sex running down my legs. Having slept naked, the silhouette of my voluptuous 183lbs was visible on the wall as I walked around the bed, in the dimly lit room.

"Damn, baby, you left a puddle on your side," Omar let out. He wasn't telling me anything that I didn't already know. When rubbed the right way, this super soaker had a mind of her own.

"It be like that sometimes," was all I could say as I left the room to shower in the hallway bathroom.

There was a bathroom in my bedroom that I could've used but I needed to come down off my sex high in peace. I didn't want to have to think about the man's feelings on the other side of the door, my man. I'd gotten caught up in another wet dream. This one being more intense than the last. The six foot four, peanut butter skin toned, furry browed, brown-eyed, no-nonsense Cameron had invaded my home and made his way into my dreams once again. I couldn't shake his fine ass.

"Get it together, Cam," I spoke to myself in the mirror. *"Don't make no damn sense lusting over no man like that. And you,"* I cast my eyes downward to address my kitty. *"You need to get a grip. Well... I mean, your grip isn't the issue...but, you know what I mean. Behave."* Giving my phat ma a light smack, my clit responded. Throwing my head back, I bit my lip. I was such a damn freak.

Shaking my head, I leaned over and turned on the shower. While I felt wrong for having secret sex that had been reserved for my dreams over the last six months, it was only through those dreams that I was able to reach my orgasmic peak. Omar couldn't keep up with my sex drive, nor keep my salacious sexual appetite fed. I wanted every inch of my body explored. I wanted a nigga to sign his name on this pussy. And though I wanted Omar to be the man for the job, at 31 years young, I couldn't see myself teaching any man how to please me.

Often, I found myself wondering if the mediocre sex was enough to chuck the deuces on him but always talked myself out of calling it quits. I was strongly opposed to going through the whole *getting to know you* phase with anyone else. I'd given Omar a hard enough time in the beginning of our relationship, so in a way, I felt obligated to see it through. We met in a small coffee shop a year ago and I was just twenty-four hours fresh off a breakup. I'd spent the previous night packing up my ex-boyfriend of five years belongings after deciding I was tired of housing a bum with good dick and no ambition.

It was crazy how I let good dick cloud my judgment for that long, but it was a lesson learned. While Omar's smile was genuine and his pick-up lines unique, I wasn't going for it and shut down his request for my number as soon as it passed his lips. Seeing him a few more times at the coffee shop after that, his persistence eventually wore me down. After two months of courting, we began dating exclusively. Once it was solidified, I put the pussy on him that night. And that night, I found out that the dick wasn't hittin' on shit.

Still, I put my need for mind-blowing sex to the side. Even if I had to find other ways to get myself off. Wet dreams and keeping my rose in my nightstand as well as my purse in case I ever felt the need to take the edge off had become a thing. Now, I was far from a nympho, but sex for me was just as important in a relationship as communication. And that may sound crazy, considering I couldn't communicate to my man that his sex was a three and a half on a one to ten scale. Sighing, I hopped in the shower and washed myself from head to toe twice before stepping out and into my towel.

Drying off, I wrapped the towel tightly around my body and went back to the room. Thankfully, Omar was fast asleep. I didn't want him to see me leave the room after slipping on my panties and a T-shirt. He was a cuddler and I didn't feel right cuddling up with him after the dream I'd had. I also didn't enjoy sleeping in the wet spot.

Grabbing my phone and tumbler filled with ice water from the nightstand, I quietly crept out and made my way to the living room. I had a good two hours before I had to get up and get ready for work. Unfolding the Ugg throw blanket that lay across the couch, I covered myself up with it and closed my eyes. Sleep came easy, as it often did after a good orgasm. And though I felt wrong for having them, I had to admit that the wet dreams were good for the body.

"OKAY, and what did you do after that?" My best friend, Janell asked as we caught up on our morning FaceTime call while I drove to work.

"After my shower, I threw some clothes on and went to the living room to sleep."

"Bitch, you did what?!" She jumped up from her desk, knocking her chair over. She was as dramatic as she was loyal. **"Hold on, lemme close this door before my students come in."**

Janell was a sixth-grade ELA teacher at a Charter school. One would have never known that the Howard University grad had such a foul mouth and a thing for women by the way she carried herself. I knew, though. We had been best friends since high school and inseparable. People often speculated about us bumping coochies because it was rare that you saw me without her and vice versa. It didn't help that she was open about her love for the female anatomy. But still, I didn't let the rumors bother me. Janell was my ace.

"Yeah, or the principal."

"Girl, ain't nobody scared of that old white lady. Any who, please tell me why you thought it was okay to fall into a peaceful slumber, on the couch after being fucked by another man in your dreams."

"What else would you have had me do that would've made more sense, Nell?"

"Fuck him, Camille. You were supposed to fuck yo' man and any doubt that may have crept into his mind."

"Didn't I tell you he thought it was him in the dream?"

"All the more reason to have fucked the shit out of him so the thought remained." She sighed. "You being friends with me this long and actin' like you don't know how to think ahead is rather appalling."

"Girl shut up, wasn't nobody doing all that. He was asleep once I was out of the shower. Back to the reason I called, though. The dreams are becoming more frequent and I'm about to lose my damn mind. This gotta be some kind of sign."

The school bell could be heard in the background, signaling the end of our conversation.

"Drinks and dinner at my house later?"

"I'd love to, babes. And I'm spending the night."

"So, you can wet up my sheets, I think not." She put her hand up to her mouth to hide her laugh.

"I would call you out your name, but I'm gonna save it for later. Have a great day, heaux."

"And you have a splendid one, Ms. Wet Wet." She blew me a kiss and disconnected the call.

Pulling into the employee parking lot of Fishkill Correctional Facility, I parked in my assigned spot. Taking the keys out of the ignition, I put my iPad in my purse and grabbed my tea. As the Unit Manager at the all-male facility, I was responsible for conducting daily rounds of my unit to pinpoint security breaches, reviewing inmate behavior logs, etc. to ensure compliance with the facility. I'd worked at the prison for four years and had just entered my second year in the position. Moving up in the ranks so quickly wasn't a surprise, seeing as I had all the great qualities of a leader.

It also helped that the inmates in my unit rocked with me heavily. I'd been assigned to what the inmates called a "thunder dorm". Things could pop off at any given time and they had, but once I was put in position, the unit had done a 180. Not only did I give the guys the same respect as I gave anyone on the outside, but I gave them something to look at. Standing at five foot six, I was a thick woman.

From my ample breasts to the pudge around my stomach, down to my thick hips and round ass, the men awaited my walkthrough Monday through Friday. With a round face, my eyes, nose, and chin were perfectly proportioned. My skin tone mirrored the color of Jack Daniels liquor, and my face had a permanent glow due to my daily skincare routine. I loved my job, interacting with the people that society had cast away on some levels. Though I had a few battles here and there with the men who wanted to throw their weight around, the good outweighed the bad for the most part.

Using my badge, I entered Unit H and greeted the officers who'd worked the overnight shift and went straight to my office. Setting my bag down, I powered up my computer to check my emails and to-do list for the day. There was so much to be done over the span of eight hours, but I made sure to never leave work left over for the next day.

I prided myself on being efficient and it showed every time I went up for review with the warden. Grabbing my blinged-out clipboard, I walked out onto the compound to do my daily walkthrough. Typically, the men would be out of their cells, moving about freely, but they'd been on lockdown for the last week due to an altercation that resulted in a stabbing. I hated to make everyone pay for the actions of two individuals, but rules were rules, and there was but so much leeway I could give. My first stop was the control room.

"Hey, Dave. How were my men last night?" I asked one of the officers who often had issues in the unit because of his attitude.

"Quiet for the most part but you know there's always a select few that want to act an ass to prove something to the rest of the lowlifes."

My face formed a small smile as I asked for the names of the inmates he was referring to so I could jot them down. I wasn't smiling because I agreed with his statement, but I had mastered the art of killing people with kindness. He read off a list of four names and I nodded. "Thanks." Turning to leave, I paused to address him again. "You know, if you weren't so aggressive in your approach, maybe you'd have a different result. Yes, we want to be stern, but when it gets to being a dick-swinging contest, that's where we fall short."

Dave gave a nod of contempt, followed by a forced smile. "I'll keep that in mind."

"Sounds good." I was good for having the last word.

Leaving the control room, I headed back out to start my rounds and speak with the guys Dave mentioned.

"Aye, Ms. D, I need to holla atchu' for a second."

"Ms. D, they need to fix the heat in here."

"You looking good today, Ms. D."

"Ms. D, they didn't take my sto' sheet yesterday."

As I went to each cell, there was a different request, grievance, or some kind of compliment being thrown at me. I spoke to everyone, making sure to write down every issue, even if I felt it was ridiculous or an outright lie. Once I'd gone through the top tier, I did the same with the bottom. Reaching the last cell, I took a deep breath before calling out to the inmate. He was the last person Dave had named on his list and one that stayed to himself for the most part.

He was transferred to the facility six months ago and it didn't take long for him to learn the ropes and establish himself. He was a loner for sure, but the inmates seemed to gravitate to him. Respectful, he demanded respect in return from inmates and staff alike.

"Haynes," I called out to him, and he appeared at the window a few seconds later. "How's it going?"

"Why do you insist on calling me, Haynes?" His authoritative yet sexy tone made me suck in a breath. Taking in his almond-colored skin, perfectly chiseled jawline, suckable lips, and alluring eyes, I unconsciously shifted from side to side, feeling my nipples harden.

Gathering myself, I hid my true feelings behind a professional smile. "I call you by your last name like everyone else here."

"I ain't everyone else in here, though. I'm Cameron." He rubbed his low-cut fade and his lips curled into a small smile.

His name sounded even better coming from him than the times I'd cried it out during one of my toe-curling orgasms. He was Cameron Haynes; the inmate that had hijacked my inner thoughts and dreams.

Chapter 2

CAMERON

This lockdown shit was blowin' me. Again, the whole dorm had to suffer behind two junkies who decided to stab it out over some fuckin' meth. These niggas were constantly fighting over drugs they didn't buy, and the shit was mind-boggling to me. What was even more tragic than the bunch of junkies that occupied the dorm was the number of so-called hustlers. I watched these niggas get their cups of tobacco, cups of gas, pills, and whatever else they could get smuggled in, only to turn around and sell it for status and a couple of zebra cakes. Out of the whole dorm, there were probably three dudes, outside of myself, that were talkin' bout something. Other than that, this shit was a cesspool of rejects.

I'd just entered the last sixty days of a five-year sentence for assault and battery but had been at Fishkill for the last six months. It was hands down the most bummed-out camp I'd been to. Unfortunately for me, in some instances, I had no choice but to deal with the people around me. The same people I'd never allow myself to cross paths with on the streets. I mainly stayed to myself, only seen when business was involved. I was lucky to have a cell all to myself, that way I didn't have to engage with any of these niggas. A man of few words, I preferred it that way.

This wasn't my first time behind the wall, but it was the longest, and would most certainly be my last. Thanks to my airhead-ass baby mother, I'd been hit with assault charges after pistol-whipping her brother for spanking my one-year-old daughter at the time. While her brother had ultimately committed the act, I was more pissed at her for trying to defend the nigga when I pulled up. She knew what the result would be once she called to let me know what had gone down. And truthfully, had it not been for my brother pulling me away and my daughter's cries, that nigga would've seen the bright light and taken a walk with Jesus.

The only reason I didn't get more time was because of the bruise my daughter had on her back as a result of the spanking. And even as they handed down my sentence, I still let it be known that I had a bullet with his name on it. Prison wasn't the place for a trill nigga such as myself. While I was able to continue my business behind the wall to a certain extent, I'd much rather be in the free world with my people. The only upside I'd seen to this place besides the endless junkies shopping my product, was seeing the unit manager's face five days a week.

The day I arrived in the dorm, she was the first person I met. As she gave me a rundown on how things ran in what she called "her unit", all I could think about was her pretty, pink lips wrapped around my dick, and my hand on the back of her head, guiding her as she sucked me up. The sticky shit on her lips, with the brown tint, was the perfect combo that made her mouth form into the perfect pout. While I could've pushed up on her out the gate, the same way I was sure these other niggas had, I played it lowkey.

For the last few months, I'd been doing subtle flirting here and there. It was just enough to let her know that I saw her, but not too much to have her spooked. I wanted to fuck her thick ass in the worse way, though. I loved thick women, especially the ones who carried themselves well. Ms. D didn't dress in prison uniform like the C.O's, she wore street clothes. I took note of how she filled out her slacks and kept her collared shirts buttoned up just enough for the titty meat to be exposed.

"I know you're Cameron," she spoke, pulling my attention back to where she stood, outside my cell door. "But I don't do special treatment, Haynes. You should know that by now." Batting her naturally long eyelashes, she smirked at me.

"Yeah, I know, but them other niggas don't make you blush like I do, Ms. D. You like coming to visit a nigga cell, huh?"

"I go to every cell, Haynes. It's my job," she countered with a slick smile.

"True, but you in and out with them. When you come over here, you linger. And don't get me wrong, I ain't complaining. I just want you to know that I know."

Pulling her clipboard to her chest, she cocked her head to the side. "And what is it that you think you know?"

It was now my turn to smirk. "I know you wanna fuck wit a nigga. You want me to pull you in this cell and stroke that pussy. I know that shit phat, too. Bet the clit play peekaboo through the lips and shit." Putting my arm up on the door, I leaned my head against it. "Just know that I'm wit it whenever you ready and don't nobody gotta know. I'll tear dat ass up anywhere you'd like, on soul."

Her face and neck became flush, confirming the accuracy of my statement. Ms. D wanted a nigga to put a hurtin' on that thang. She cleared her throat and straightened her posture. "Can you tell me what happened between you and Officer Dave?"

I shrugged. "Ain't nothin' to tell."

Officer Dave, whom the dorm referred to as, Officer Dickhead, had let a little authority go to his head and didn't know how to talk to people. There wasn't a day that went by where I didn't hear or see him going at it with another inmate after he started some shit. It was his thing to get niggas riled up just to complain to whoever would listen when they went at him.

"Well, he says different."

"Take his side, then."

"Y'all can't be giving him a reason to complain, especially when I'm vouching for y'all."

"That's his thing, ma. Think about it, we been on lock-down, what the hell can we do behind the door that would warrant static with this clown?" She went quiet. "Exactly. He comes to do the count and just get to talkin' crazy. Just cause we in these state greens it doesn't change the fact that we're men and demand respect. Well, I can only speak for myself. I ain't going for nobody talkin' to me crazy, ma."

"Ms. D," she corrected me.

"You should let me put this d in you."

Smiling, she shook her head. "I'll have a talk with Officer Dave so we can get this figured out, okay. I'm sure you don't want a write-up on your file. Especially with you on your way out of here."

"Don't make me no never mind. So long as he keeps on the bullshit, I'ma have the same energy. Besides, I know the write-up gon' guarantee me a seat in yo office." I licked my lips. "And the more times I'm in there, it's another opportunity to get **in there**." I glanced downward and bit my lip.

"Good day, Mr. Haynes," she said, making a note on her paper before turning to leave.

"Ay, hol' up." Pivoting, she cocked her head to the side, waiting for me to speak. "I like the braids better."

"What?"

"Your hair. I mean, you look good in that ponytail, too, but I like the long braids better. Get those again the next time you go get your hair done."

"Good day, Mr. Haynes," she repeated before switching off.

From my window, I watched her hips sway as she walked across the dorm and to her office which I had a direct view of. As she entered the office, she turned and locked eyes with me before slowly closing the door behind her. Curling my lip up in a smirk, I nodded. I was gon' get that pussy. She knew it and I knew it, too.

Grabbing my phone from the spot I'd created in the cell to hold my work, I powered it on and tapped the Instagram app. Every now and then, I went on the app and scrolled from my dummy account for about thirty minutes. It was my way of keeping in touch with the outside world outside of my family. While scrolling, I came across Ms. D's account. I'd found her page through my sister-in-law's sister who Ms. D was best friends with.

She didn't know that I'd done my research on her my first month in the joint. I don't even think my sister-in-law thought I was serious when I asked for a rundown on what she was about. Being the chatty person she was, she gave me all I needed to know without divulging Ms. D's full life story.

Having access to her IG page where she often posted, I'd jacked my dick to her pretty ass face plenty of nights. I loved ass, titties, and pussy just as much as the next man, but there was something about a pretty ass smile, on a pretty ass mouth. It often made me wonder if you could tell if a woman had pretty pussy lips by the lips on her face. It was just a thought at the end of the day, but goddamn. With her big, plumped lips, I knew her dick-sucking skills were A1. I knew an eater when I saw one.

I scrolled through her most recent posts and just as I got ready to rub one out to her face, the phone vibrated in my hand, with a FaceTime call from my daughter's mother. I knew Sarai was in school, so whatever her reason for calling was, it likely didn't have anything to do with our kid. Still, I plugged my earbuds in to answer the call.

The call connected and I was greeted by Destiny's moans and her fingers slipping in and out of her bald pussy. My dick rocked up instantly, and I wasted no time springing it free from my white, state boxers.

"Mmm, Cam, this pussy is so wet for you, baby," she cooed while spreading her legs further apart, allowing me to see her wetness drip down to her ass. **"I miss you so much."**

I tuned Destiny out and focused on the pussy only. Cracking open a brand-new jar of Vaseline, I coated my dick with a thin layer and went to stroking. **"Mmm, open them lips up for me,"** I instructed.

She spread her pussy lips, allowing me to get a good look at her pink flesh. **"Like this, baby?"**

"Yeah, just like that. Spread them thighs and let me get up in there. Oohhh, shit yeah, gimmie that pussy." I stroked my dick at a medium pace, thinking about having Ms. D's legs wrapped around my waist as I pounded her shit.

Destiny rubbed her clit feverishly and I could see it swell up. It was clear that she'd been at it before calling me. And since I didn't really fuck with her, I wasn't about to give her the satisfaction of cummin' before me, so I sped up my strokes.

"Arghhh, shit," I groaned, focusing on the head of my dick, feeling my nut building.

"Yeah, baby daddy, gimmie dat big ass dick." Moving the phone from her pussy, she put it on her face.

"Put it back down," I demanded. Pouting, she slowly turned the phone back down so that I had an eyeful of pussy again. Letting out a throaty groan, I gave my dick two more strokes before releasing in my hand. **"Ooouu, ooouu, shit."** Sighing, I ended the call and put the phone down next to me.

Taking a few moments to regain my energy, I got up to clean myself off. After rinsing my hands, the phone rang again. It was Destiny, only this time it was an audio call.

"Wassup."

"I see I still got it," she boasted. **"That dick miss me, don't he?"**

"Don't flatter yourself. I've been in this bitch for four

years. It don't take much from a woman to get my shit hard. I can buss a nut to a bad bitch in a turtleneck, Des. Seeing some throwback pussy gets the same reaction."

The other end of the phone went silent, signaling that I'd deflated her ego or pissed her off. I was cool with either one.

"You know, sometimes I really don't like you."

"Same. Why you calling me if my baby ain't witchu?" Checking myself out in the cracked mirror that hung above the sink, the only thing that changed about me over the years was the beard I'd grown out.

"I called because I had a dream about you last night and woke up horny. Knowing you get up early, I figured I'd try my luck."

"Yeah, you caught me at a good time." Taking my toothbrush and toothpaste from my box, I brushed my teeth.

"Seeing that chocolate stick got me thinkin' bout old times."

Spitting out the toothpaste and going for the second round of brushing, I paused to end the call. "If that's all, we can go ahead and wrap this up."

"Wait, before you hang up, I wanted to know if—."

"No, you can't come see me, Des." I already knew what she was gonna ask before she could finish her sentence.

She sucked her teeth, letting out a loud sigh. "It's been four years, Cam, I said I was sorry."

"And I heard you, but your sorry can't turn back the hands of time and get me those years back with Sarai. I missed four years of her life and now I gotta settle for seeing my baby for a few hours every Saturday. You'll never understand that shit. So, no, you can't come see me 'cause we ain't on that no mo' and I ain't tryna give you no false hope. Respect my decision and let's keep things as they are."

"Alright, Cameron. I'm not gonna beg you no more. I'll just make sure Sarai gets to your mom's house tonight for tomorrow's visit."

"Preciate that, Fantasia. You and that pussy have a good day." I cleared the line and prepared for another day behind the wall. I hoped like hell that the lockdown was lifted, a nigga needed some sunlight and a quick lap around the yard.

Chapter 3

CAMILLE

I'd spent more than half of my day in my office, even working through lunch. I'd been going through paperwork, reclassifying the inmates in my unit based on their recent interactions with each other as well as the staff assigned to the unit. Each inmate file was organized in alphabetical order by last name and in reaching for the letter H, Cameron Haynes was at the top. Opening the manilla folder, his mugshot greeted me. He wore a straight expression in the picture, but his stare was so intense, that I found myself analyzing his facial structure. The man was well crafted from his well-defined jawline to his full lips, proportioned nose, and mesmerizing dark eyes. Cameron didn't need to be told how fine he was.

It was hard not to get sucked in when he spoke in a calm tone that commanded attention without him having to utter a harsh word. Locked in with the photo, I absentmindedly played with my ponytail. It was clear that he was watching me just as hard as I watched him to even mention my knotless braids. Crossing my legs, I pulled my bottom lip into my mouth and my teeth sunk into it. Thoughts of Cameron bending me over my desk, his hand over my mouth, stroking me slowly invaded my mind.

I shuddered at the imagery. Letting out a deep sigh, I went to set his file to the side. Hearing my phone vibrate, I opened my desk drawer and reached for it. It was Omar calling for his daily check-in. It was his routine to check on me after lunch.

"Hey, babe," I answered in a chipper tone.

"Hey, beautiful. How's your day going?"

"Busy as usual, but good overall. How bout you?"

"Same. We got a new contract today, so you know I have some long nights ahead of me."

Omar worked as a contractor for Hilton Hotels. Working for a popular hotel chain had its perks, and I couldn't tell you how many times I'd suggested a staycation with O just so we could feast on each other. We'd yet to make it happen and that bummed me out sometimes. There was nothing like spontaneous sex or sex outside of your home in general. Unfortunately, things like that didn't excite him.

"Congratulations, Big Money."

He chuckled. **"Man, go head."**

"Yes!" I blurted out, excited about the email that I'd received from the prison's warden.

"Sounds like you have good news also."

"I do. It came through at the right time, too. Let me go, baby so I can handle this."

"Okay, I love you. See you at home."

"I love you, too. Oh, and I'm going to Janelle's for a girl's night. So, I'll be home to change and grab a few things."

"Damn, aight. I wanted to do some things to you tonight."

"Oh, really? Do tell." Leaning back in my chair, I ran my tongue over my top lip. I was always down for some freak shit, even if it was in conversation.

"I planned to…"

"Aye, O, we need you out front," I heard someone call out to him in the background, putting an end to what would've been at least a good 30 seconds of nasty talk. That was all Omar could do before it got awkward on his end.

"Sorry bout that, baby. I'm gonna text you."

"All good."

Ending the call, I set my phone back down on my desk.

It vibrated again, but only once, indicating a text message notification. Figuring it was Omar, I picked it up. A message notification from a 347 number on WhatsApp appeared on the screen. I rarely used the app, so getting a message through it was odd. Being that the number wasn't saved and didn't look familiar, I hesitated to check it. My phone wasn't set up to show previews of my messages from the app, so I was prompted to open it. I wasn't prepared for the message and video attachment.

347-248-5982: *This could be yours but you playin'.*

Pressing play on the video, it was dark for a few seconds before the most beautiful, brown dick I'd ever seen appeared on the screen. I watched as a tattooed hand stroked the dick, stopping at the mushroom tip and giving it a squeeze. The pre cum oozed out of it, causing a low moan to escape my lips. Zooming in to get a better look, I was able to make out the name tattooed on the hand that read Sarai. It was Cameron. Just as I went to rewind the video back to the beginning, a knock at my door made me jump, and the phone hit the floor with a loud smack.

"Uhhh, umm, who is it?" I fumbled with my words, bending over to pick up my phone and inspect it for damages.

"It's Kayla," I heard from the other side of the door.

"Come in." Throwing the phone in my desk drawer, I stood up.

"Hey, did you get that email?" Kayla was an LT that I was cool with. She'd shown me the ropes when I started as a C.O.

"Yeah. I was just about to come out there." I shifted my weight from one leg to the other, feeling antsy and nervous as if she had a way of knowing what I was doing only a few minutes before her visit.

"I know they gon' be geeked to come off this lockdown. We haven't gone this long in a minute. I hope they don't fuck it up."

"They won't," I assured her.

She snickered. "You be having so much faith in them, knowing they be cuttin' up."

"They do, but it's not all of them."

"Yeah, you're right about that. They've been chill for the most part, but you know being locked down makes them antsy. The only person we know for sure ain't gon' be in no shit is Haynes."

My head popped up and I gave her my undivided attention. "What, how you figure we know that?" I questioned, immediately regretting the alarm in my tone.

"Cause he stays in his cell. You okay?" She inquired with a raised brow.

I wanted to say, *no I'm not okay. I'm thinkin' about risking it all and letting an inmate wear this good pussy out,* but instead, responded with, "Yeah, girl, I'm fine. Why you ask?"

"You sure? Your face looks a little flushed."

"Oh, it's a little warm in here. You not hot?" I pulled at the color of my shirt.

"No, I'm good. I'ma head back out front. Remember, don't let these men in here get to you, girl."

I'm about to let one of these niggas get up in me, I thought to myself while glancing down at my drawer where my phone was tucked away. "You know I won't."

Nodding, she left my office. Scared that I'd be tempted to watch the video again or even worse, respond to the text, I didn't bother reaching for the phone. Cameron had me discombobulated from just wanting to feel the tip of the dick. Feeling my pussy juicing up, I ignored the urge to lock my office door, prop my legs up on the arms of my chair, and let my rose strum my clit until I leaked all over the seat. I was completely enamored with inmate #95A768.

THE IMAGE of Cameron stroking his dick still hadn't left my mind even after my shift ended and I was headed home. My mouth salivated just thinking about the things I could do with my tongue that would surely make his toes curl and ears ring. I was so in my head that I didn't notice that I'd missed my exit and was now headed in the direction of Janelle's house, which was about thirty minutes from mine.

"Ahh, what the hell," I said out loud, continuing on. I kept gym clothes in my trunk, so I'd change into those. Being that I would be arriving at Nell's house earlier than I planned to, I called her to let her know. Her phone rang a couple of times before she answered.

"Hey, boo."

"Hey, girl. Tell me why I missed my exit on the way home."

"How the hell you miss the exit you take every day, Cam?"

"I was in my head and clearly zoned out. I didn't know I passed it until I noticed I was two exits from your place. You home?"

She chuckled. "Bitch, keep it 100, you were in your head about that nigga, wasn't you?"

"Are you home?" I dodged her question.

"Shit, now I wanna see his fine ass myself. What's his DIN number so I can look him up."

"I am not giving you all that. Are you home or not, Nell?" Her ass always did the most.

"Not yet. KK is there, though. She having man problems and needed a girl's night, too."

"Okay, I'll see you there then."

"Alright, drive safe, Ms. I Can't Help But To Have Dick On The Brain."

"I'm hanging up now," I announced before doing just that.

Before I could set my phone down in the center console, it rang in my hand. With a quick glance at the caller ID, I noticed it was an incoming call from the 347 number. Quickly, declining the call, I threw my phone down in the passenger seat like it was infected.

"This nigga is too bold," I said out loud to myself.

I wasn't even surprised that he had access to a cell phone. I was almost positive that most of the inmates in the unit had one. They were very resourceful. While we worked tirelessly to get the contraband under control, it would take more than the staff at Fishkill to do so. It was a widespread thing amongst the prisons around the country. And so long as I didn't see it, I didn't say anything.

FINALLY MAKING it to Nell's apartment, I parked and grabbed my gym bag from my trunk. I was so cap because the bag was a façade. I'd only used it twice after convincing myself that I would work out at least four times a week; before and after work. After the second day, I hung that *New Year, New Me* bullshit up real quick, cause gym who? Taking the two flights upstairs, I could hear Tamar Braxton's "All The Way Home" blasting from Nell's apartment. Using the spare key she'd given me, I stuck it in the door and pushed it open.

"Don't even know what we're fighting for, damn I need a minute, so, baby, keep your distance. I heard it all, so I'ma just go. Don't bother waiting up, I just need some time alone."

Nell's sister, Akira stood in the middle of the living room belting out the lyrics as if she wrote them herself. Closing the door behind me, I locked it and proceeded to yell out her name.

"KK!" Startled, she jumped and turned in my direction.

Smiling, I waved, and she turned the music down to a decent volume. "What Keion do?" I asked about her fiancé as I went to give her a hug.

"Nothing but get on my damn nerves." She sucked her teeth before embracing me.

"Y'all are a mess. Come on, let's raid the bar and we can talk about it while we wait on Nell." I dropped my bag on the couch, and we went to the bar that Nell had set up in her living room.

As she went to speak, I heard keys in the door. Pulling out a bottle of Don Julio, I got a shot glass for each of us.

"Welcome home, seester," KK greeted.

"What it do, boo. Damn, y'all was about to drink without a bitch, in my own house? Where is the respect?" I laughed, poured the shots, and held hers up for her to take. "My girl." She kissed KK's cheek and blew a kiss at me. "What we toasting to?"

"A long overdue girls' night," I said, with my glass in the air.

"Love," KK added with a smile.

"Booooo, no to both of those," Nell shut us down. "Let's make a toast to me being a bad bitch and being promoted to Dean at my school today."

"Ahhhhhh," me and KK let out at the same time, setting our glasses down and bum rushing Nell.

"Congratulations, bitchhhh!!!"

"Thanks, doll."

"Siss, that is so great. You'sa bad bitch, you know that," KK hyped her.

"When you right, you right." Nell raised her shot glass in the air before throwing her drink back like a pro.

"Okay, okay, now we really gotta celebrate. Damn, I gotta go home and get some clothes."

"No, I wanna chill inside. Besides, I already celebrated," she said, taking her jacket off and tossing it on the couch.

"Celebrated with who? When? Where? How?" KK asked.

"You know I hate when you get to asking eight questions in one sentence, KK. I celebrated with Tia, tonight, in the backseat of my car, with my pussy in her mouth. Another shot, please."

"You know whatttt, you something else," I let out while taking my shot and refilling hers. Tia was Nell's consistent fuck buddy who she claimed she didn't want anything serious with. I never tried to convince her to admit that she wanted more even though I knew she did.

"If I'm something else, then you something else," she countered with a wink.

"Whatever."

"You know I hate when y'all talk over my head," KK interjected, and I snickered. "Now, I know why she something else," she pointed to Nell, "but what's going on with you?" She faced me.

"Nothing." Pouring myself a double shot, I threw it back.

"Oh, a double shot, huh? Y'all betta spill right now."

"Cam has been dreaming about fucking one of the inmates in her unit for the past six months," Nell blurted out.

KK's mouth flew open, and her eyes grew wide.

"Damn bitch, how you know I wanted it to come out like that."

"I thought he was just asking about you out of the blue," KK whispered.

"Huh, he who?" I questioned.

"Ummm…"

"Ummm, my ass. Who is he and why is he asking about me?"

Without answering me, KK got up and walked over to the couch. I looked at Nell who shrugged her shoulders, like she was just as clueless as me.

I watched as KK's fingers moved across the screen of her phone before walking back over to us. She wore an apologetic look on her face. "Okay, look, before you get mad about what I'm about to tell you, know that my intentions were pure. At the time I didn't put two and two together because who would even think—."

"You stalling, Akira."

"And talkin' fast," Nell pointed out. "Why would she be mad?"

"Is this the guy at your prison?" She slowly held the phone up and Cameron's sexy mug was on the screen.

"Okayyy, why you showing her a picture of Keion's brother?"

"Keion's brother?!" I exclaimed.

"Yeah, that's Cam…oh shit. Girl, this the dude?"

I nodded. "Yes. That's Cameron Haynes, the one I've been telling you about. Wait, KK, you gave him my number?!"

"No, no. He asked about you a few months ago after seeing your picture on my page and stuff. You know, he said you were fine, and you know me, I'm always looking for an opportunity to brag on my bitches. So, I told him a little bit about you. I didn't tell him where you worked or anything."

"But, KK, you know he's housed at Fishkill, you didn't put two and two together?" What she was saying sounded so off. I wasn't mad but I was very confused and even more shocked.

"Nah, I didn't. I don't ask those kinds of questions. All I know is he's locked up and he and Keion speak every other day. And like I said, I only told him a little bit about you. With his connections, he could've done his own research. I'm sorry, boo." She poked her lip out and I waved her off.

"You don't have to be sorry," Nell finally spoke again. "She's been having the best sex of her life, even if it's in her dreams."

"Shut up, Nell."

"I will not be hushed in my own home." She crossed her arms and held her head up to the sky, making KK laugh.

"She gets on my nerves sometimes." I couldn't help but laugh myself.

"The best sex, though, Cam? It's like that?" KK leaned in on the bar like she wanted to know more.

"Now that I know who it is, I'm not even surprised. That nigga Cam gives Big Dick Energy a whole new meaning. If I was into what y'all was into I'd give that nigga some and do the nine-month bid after. Take the maternity pictures and all, shiiddd. Be out this bitch posing like Sexyy Red."

"That dick big alright," I said under my breath, thinkin' about the video I'd moved to the hidden folder in my phone.

"Say what now?" Of course, Nell would pick up on what I said. "You seen it already? Bitch, you holdin' out?"

"Unh, unh, I can't be listening to this. That's my brother-in-law." KK put her hands up to her ears.

"Well, he ain't mine," Nell let out. "Go head and order dinner cause we gon' talk about this." KK walked off again, and Nell stared me down. "Soooo, have you seen the dick?"

"Grab my phone."

"Grab yo phone?" She repeated, with her lip curled up.

"Yes, it's in my purse." As if I wasn't already feeling the other shots I'd taken, I poured another.

The revelation of how close Cameron was to my circle was a lot. Nell went to do as I said and held my phone out for me to take. Seeing a missed call from O, I went to call him back first. I was sure that he was reaching out to see if I'd reached Nell's. The phone rang twice before going to voicemail. Sending him a text, I let him know that I was good and to give me a call when he got a minute. Exiting our thread, I went to WhatsApp and opened the thread for the 347 number.

"Okay, so you wanted me to bring you your phone for what?" Nell pressed.

"For this." I set the phone down on the bar and slowly slid it to her. "Read the message then press play." I waited a few seconds for her reaction and got just what I thought I would from my crazy friend.

She looked up at me with a sneaky smile and said, "Okay, do you want me to do the recording when you send yours so you can get the right angle, or you got it? I ain't trippin' bout seeing ya coochie, I've seen it before and she pretty. And we both know that says a lot coming from me."

I snatched my phone from her and snickered. "Girl, I ain't sending nothing back. And you having an image of my cat in your head is wild, Nell."

"It's not even like that, so relax. And why are you not responding?"

"Cause...cause I got a man, Janelle."

"And I get that, monogamy is a beautiful thing, but have you seen **that** beautiful thing in your phone."

"Yes, I have, and I will admire it from afar."

"Ooh, girl you suck. I don't wanna hear another word about how you're not being fucked right."

"Then you'll have officially lost your best friend cool points. You're supposed to listen to my problems and come up with a solution. That's best friend code."

"Girl, bye. The best friend code is to not let you and Ms. Wet Wet suffer. Now, I don't know Cameron that well but the few times I've been around him, he seems cool. I don't see him telling. Plus, he a real street nigga, it's against their ethics. The way I see it, you either teach O how to fuck you right, or you get to abusing yo power so Cam can punish that pussy. The choice is yours, my girl." She grabbed the bottle of Don Julio, glanced at my phone once more, and went to walk off. "Dick look so goddamn yummy, got me all wet. I'm going to my room real quick, and when I say real quick, I mean ten minutes. I gotta go get my mind right."

I knew her nasty ass was only going to call Tia so they could fuck on FaceTime. With my phone still open to Cam's message, I played the video again. I knew I couldn't cross the line. I was afraid that if I did, we'd be so hooked on each other there would be no turning back.

CAMERON

Once the cell doors were popped, letting us know that the lockdown had been lifted, traffic was steady at the trap. Every time a nigga pulled up, they knew to talk money and money only. Anything else was a waste of my time. And seeing as I'd already given the state enough of that, I didn't have any to spare for niggas just wanting to shoot the shit. Hearing a knock at the cell door, I put my phone down to go to the flap. I'd just sat down to check my messages to see if Ms. D had responded to the video I'd sent her a few hours ago. I knew her scary ass had seen the video because she had her read receipts on.

"Who dat?" I called out while standing up.

"It's Casper, Omega sent me," someone responded in a deep rasp that I didn't recognize.

It was going on 11:15 p.m. and I usually shut everything down by 11 so that all my shit was put away before count time at 11:30. People that shopped with me knew that. I didn't know what this Casper dude had going on, but I was good with names and faces, and he'd never shopped with me before. Instead of leaning over to check the flap like I normally would, I spoke to him through the window.

"What he sent you for?"

He stood up so that I could see his face and my junkie meter went off immediately. And though he didn't look smoked out, I knew junkie eyes when I saw them. Omega was known to get to it just like me, only I brought in more product than him. Either way, I knew damn well he wouldn't have sent dude my way.

"I'm tryna see if I can get something on credit."

"For future reference, if you gon' use someone's name to possibly vouch for you, make sure you got yo bread up front. I don't do credit and I don't take shorts. My trap closes at 11, so go head and clear the premises. They bout to run count and a nigga ain't tryna be on lockdown again cause you choosing to bum around the dorm, looking for ways to get high for free."

"I'm sayin…" He went to speak again and was cut off by my back as I turned away from the door.

I'd said too much already. I wasn't about to sit at the door going back and forth over my policies. Sitting back down, I picked my phone up and texted Ms. D's number again. I started to write something casual like wyd, but it was late, and I wasn't about to play with her.

Me: You gon' let a nigga see that pussy, Ms. D?

The typing indicator came up and disappeared immediately. Chuckling, I sent another message.

Me: Cat got your tongue.

Sexy: You can't text my phone. I can't talk to you.

She didn't know what she'd started by responding, but she'd soon find out.

Me: You ain't gotta talk to me, let me talk to her.

Sexy: Her, who?

Me: That pussy. Hit that lil microphone near the text box in the app and let me hear her.

Sexy: Cameron.

Me: Wassup, Mama?

Sexy: I can't talk to you.

Me: We've already established that. Put your pussy on the phone.

Sexy: She's asleep.

Me: Wake her up.

Plugging in my earbuds, I hit the video button to call her. She declined the call, only for me to call right back. She answered the second call, and her background was dark, making it hard for me to see her.

"I said, I can't talk to you."

"Why you answer the phone then?"

"Cause I didn't want you to start blowing my phone up."

"Blowin' your phone up?" I snickered. "I've never been that typa nigga. Two calls is all you get out of me."

"I can't stay on this phone with you."

"Cool. Turn the light on and flip the camera."

"Camer…." The call for count cut her off.

"Hold on, don't hang up." Pulling the earbuds from my ears, I got up and went to stand at the door for count.

After confirming everyone was in their respective places, the C.O's went about their business and I went back to my bunk. Plugging the earbuds back in, I noticed that the call was still going but it was dead silent.

"Yo' ass is playing with fire," she whispered harshly.

"Pussy, please," I repeated my initial request.

"I'm gonna hang up."

"Camille," I called her by her first name, "I'm about to jack my dick. Now, I can buss to a picture of you and envision what I'd do to you if you were here, or you can hit the light and I can show you just how good I can make you feel without having to touch you. The choice is yours but know I'ma get mine either way."

Sticking my phone onto the metal post on my bunk, where I had two magnets set up, I took off my shirt. It was clear that she thought a nigga was playing because she hadn't budged, and her light remained out. Pulling my pants and boxers down enough to spring my dick free, I reached for my jar of Vaseline.

"**Wait,**" she let out softly, making my dick rise without the assistance of my hand. "**Can I say something?**"

"**Yeah. But turn yo' light on first.**"

I could hear movement and then there was light, but I still couldn't see her face, due to her having the camera facing the ceiling. Before I could say something about it, her face came into view. With a scarf wrapped around her head, her face void of makeup, and that sticky lip gloss shit that I liked, she was still beautiful to me. My eyes lingered on her face for a while before traveling downward to her titties that sat up perfectly in a black, lace bra. Licking my lips, I nodded, signaling my satisfaction. Scooping up the Vaseline, I based my dick and begin to slowly stroke it. I watched as she bit her lip and locked in on my hand movements.

"**What did you wanna say?**"

"**This is crazy.**"

"**Camille.**" My tone was stern enough to get her attention but calm enough not to ruin the moment.

"**Yes.**"

"**Lean into the camera for me, Mama.**" By the look on her face, I knew her mind said no, but her body made her move the camera closer to her face. "**Open your mouth and stick your tongue out.**" She did as I asked, further turning me on. Her tongue was long and pink, and she'd opened her mouth so wide, I could see her tonsils. "**I love me an obedi-**

ent, bitch. You feel me slapping this dick on your tongue?" I smacked my dick against my hand so that the sound could mimic what it would sound like had she been on her knees, in front of me. She nodded. **"Now what I need you to do is keep your mouth open and your tongue out while I feed you this dick, okay."**

Again, she nodded. With precision, I jacked my dick while looking directly into her lust-filled eyes.

"Mmm, damn, you got a pretty ass mouth girl. This dick be so hard for you. Ever since I laid eyes on your sexy ass, I've been fantasizing about what I could do to you in this cell." Titling her head to the side, she twirled her tongue as if she was sucking me up, pulling a moan from my lips as I focused on the head of my dick. **"Yeah, eat that dick up. That pussy wet, ain't it."**

"Uh, huh," she managed to get out, with her mouth still open, and spit sliding down her chin.

"Lemme see." This time, there was no hint of hesitation. She gracefully rose, setting her phone on the dresser stationed across from the foot of the bed. She then retreated, positioning herself on the edge of the bed. With a gentle backward glide, she reclined against the plush allure of the black satin sheets. Propping herself up on matching pillows, her figure was in full view, framed beautifully against the sheets.

Her skin was blemish-free and soft looking. Her thighs appeared to be thicker than what they looked like when she was dressed in her slacks. I continued to stroke, making sure not to go too crazy, wanting the moment to last. Spreading her legs wide, she tugged at her lace panties, moving them to the side, exposing her pussy that was just as phat as I imagined it would be. I expected it to be bald, but she had a thin layer of hair covering it that I could get with. Without being told, she slid two fingers inside her wet box, and her eyes closed, while her mouth fell open into an O.

"**Ooouu,**" she vocalized her pleasure, "**I'm so wet.**"

"**Mmmhmm, show me.**"

Taking her fingers out, she held them up for me to see. They were coated in her essence. I was so caught up in the moment, I stuck my tongue out and flicked it up and down. "**You taste good, Mama. Take them panties off. I want you to hit that pussy the way you would want me to if I was there. Take that bra off, too. I wanna see them pretty ass titties.**"

Removing both her panties and bra, she turned so that she was on her side. With her left leg flat on the bed, she raised the right one in the air, giving me a shot of her ass hole and her pink pussy.

"**Show out then, Mama.**"

Closing her eyes again, she slid both fingers back in. "**Make me cum, Cameron. Please make this pussy cream all over that dick.**" The longing in her tone made my dick harder with each stroke.

"**I got you. Open that pussy up and let me get in there.**"

"**Uhhh, shit, this feels so good.**" I watched the cream seep out of her pussy lips and down her fingers, simultaneously. **"Ooouuu, you gon' make me cum on this dick."**

"That's right, wet it up." I sped up my strokes the same as she did. **"You ready?"**

"Shit, it's cummin'." Pulling her fingers out, she rubbed her clit feverishly and scooted up the bed as she wet up the sheets.

"Arghh, fuck," I grunted, as the cum shot out of my dick and onto my stomach. **"Sssss, goddamn."** I continued to stroke and felt my body twitch a bit. Once, I'd emptied all of my seeds, my phone screen went black. She'd hung up. Laughing out loud, I got up to clean myself.

Fucking Camille via video chat wasn't going to be enough for me. I needed to feel her walls. Pulling the phone down, I sent her a goodnight text.

Me: Can't wait to do it again.

WALKING out onto the visiting room floor, I was excited to see my baby girl. I looked forward to every Saturday because I knew my mother wasn't going to miss a beat when it came down to making sure Sarai was here to see me. After doing a quick check-in with the guard at the desk that was in charge of overseeing the visits, I scanned the room for my mom. My blood boiled when I saw Destiny in the corner, waving me over. Sarai was so wrapped up in a coloring book, that she didn't notice me until Destiny tapped her and pointed in my direction.

"Daddy!" She yelled out. I closed the distance between us before she could bolt across the visiting room floor. Although the guards were pretty lenient when it came to how the kids moved on the visiting floor, I always made sure to keep Sarai's energy mid-level.

Swooping her up in my arms, I kissed her cheek. "Wassup, pretty girl."

"Nothing, I was waiting for you."

"Yeah? I've been waiting on you all week." I tickled her and she fell out in a fit of giggles.

"Hey, your mom was—." I shook my head at Destiny, and she stopped speaking.

"What you over here coloring?" I asked Sarai while taking a seat across from Destiny and sitting her on my lap. She reached for her coloring book to show me the picture. "Ahhh, shit, lemme find out you got good coordination. This is nice, princess." She'd colored a picture of Tinkerbell, perfectly within the lines.

"Thank you. You want me to color one for you, Daddy?"

"I'd love that, princess."

"Okay, I'ma get a boy book," she said, hopping down off my lap. "This one got all the girls."

I smiled and Destiny giggled. "Glad you know yo' dad ain't on no soft shit. Go ahead and hook me up." The kid's corner that they had set up in the prison was a couple of feet away, next to the photo booth. I kept my eyes on her as she walked over to it and addressed Destiny at the same time. "What you got going on, Des?"

"Your mother wasn't feeling good when I went to drop Sarai off last night, so I brought her home. I know you wouldn't have wanted to miss out on a visit, so I opted to bring her myself."

To my knowledge, I'd put in a request to have her removed from my visiting list, so how she managed to pull the visit off was beyond me. At the same time, I didn't put it past the people in here to fuck up or just completely disregard the request. Most of the personnel were lazy. She thought she was slick, using our daughter as a way to get to see me. Little did she know, that just because I was physically in her presence, I was still going to move as if she wasn't there.

At this point, she was an unwanted chaperone. Sarai returned and for the remainder of the visit, we colored, talked about things that her five-year-old brain could compute, and played the few games the prison had available that was her speed. She'd included Des in the games and of course, I put on a smile for my little one. While I was faking the whole time, I could tell that Des was eating it up. I'd had the three-hour visit down to a science and once we were down to our last five minutes, I showered Sarai with kisses and told her how much I loved her. It was always the hardest part, but I couldn't go without seeing my baby, even if it did make me sad as hell watching her leave.

"I love you, too, Daddy," she giggled as I kissed her small cheeks multiple times.

"Alright, I love you more. You be good for Mommy, and I'll see you next week with grandma, okay?"

"Okay, and don't cry." Every time she left the visit she'd say that and it made me laugh.

"Okay, I won't. You not gonna cry either, right?"

"Nope."

"Why?"

"Cause I'ma big girl," she stated with pride.

"That's right, Daddy's big girl." I gave her one last tight hug and walked over to line up with the other inmates.

Destiny didn't even bother saying goodbye and that was smart on her part. I watched as they exited and prayed that my last two months went by without a hiccup. I needed to be out there with my kid.

Back in my cell, I went straight to my phone to call my mother. She hadn't told me anything about her being sick and neither did my brother. I called her and the phone rang a couple of times before going to voicemail. I left a message, and sent her a text, letting her know that she needed to call me back ASAP, then called my brother. He answered on the first ring.

"What's good?"

"What's wrong with mommy?"

"She got covid," he said casually. "She ain't tell you?"

"No, nigga. I wouldn't have asked if she did."

"Don't call me on that bullshit, man. I ain't Des, I'll hang up on your ass." Keion was like me, so I knew he wasn't bullshittin'. "Pull into that gas station, bae."

"How long has she had covid and why she ain't tell me?"

"You know she don't like for you to worry. She tested positive yesterday. She good, though. Me and KK just came from the house. KK made her some covid tea and some soup and shit." Hearing KK's name made me think about Camille.

"Oh, aight. Wassup, KK."

"Hey, Cam. How you doing?"

"I can't complain."

"Mmmhmm. I see you found your way to my homegirl."

I smirked. "Something like that. Good lookin' on the info. Ay', bro take me off speaker real quick."

"Wassup."

"I tried to call ma but she ain't answer her phone. Did you know Destiny came up here with Sarai this morning?"

"Nah, I didn't. I know you was tight."

"What, man, pissed me off. I ain't talk to her ass the whole time, even when Sarai made us both play games with her."

He laughed. "Nigga, you fucked up for that."

"Shiiidd, call it what you want."

"Well, at least you got to see, Rai."

"Yeah, I guess. Let me get off this phone and call Mommy back, though. Love you, kidd."

"Love you, too. Ay, did shorty ever respond to your message?" He asked, referring to me texting Camille.

"Yeah, she responded all right."

"Man, get off my phone," he chuckled. "Hold your head."

"You already know." I ended the call and proceeded to call my mother back. As the phone rang, a text message came through from Camille.

Sexy: I just want you to know that last night was a one-time thing.

Me: Aight, we ain't gotta do it on video chat anymore.

I snickered as I sent the message off. The pussy was already mine for the taking. Fuck she thought this was.

CAMILLE

I read Cameron's text message for the second time, rolled my eyes, and locked my phone. I hadn't moved from my spot in Janelle's guest bedroom since I woke up earlier this morning. She must've thought I was still asleep because she hadn't knocked on the door or texted my phone. It was a good thing, too. I was still trying to process last night's virtual fuck session with Cameron. Somewhere in between, *we can't do this,* and *this is wrong,* I found myself with my legs cocked open, playing with my pussy at his direction. I knew the moment I picked up his second video call that I had opened Pandora's box.

I'd halfway let him turn me out and I'd be a bald-faced lie if I said I didn't enjoy every second of it. I happily slept in my juices after ending the call with him and woke up craving more. The guilt that I was expecting to have was nonexistent. I needed the release, even if it was a one-time thing, which I'd explained to him in my text message. Only, he wasn't trying to hear that. And if the way he spoke to me last night and his response this morning was any indication of how he planned to move going forward, a bitch was in trouble.

Suddenly remembering that I hadn't heard from Omar after missing his call yesterday, I went to call him back. He hadn't crossed my mind not one time last night and that wasn't a good sign at all. The phone rang a couple of times before he finally picked up.

"**Hello,**" he answered in a groggy tone.

"**Hey, baby. My bad, I didn't mean to wake you.**"

"**You good, bae. I need to get up anyway. What time is it?**"

Moving the phone from my ear, to check the time, there was a message from Cameron. Deciding not to open it just yet, I focused back on Omar. "**It's 12:58.**"

"**Damn, I was knocked out. I got in late last night and ended up crashing on the couch. I meant to hit you back, but I didn't want to interrupt your night out with the ladies. How was it?**"

"**It was good. We celebrated Nell's promotion.**"

"Oh, that's wassup," he responded through a yawn. **"Shit."**

"Not you yawning and it's one in the afternoon."

We both laughed. The way Omar slept, you would think he had someone pregnant somewhere.

"I know, shit crazy."

Hearing a knock at the door, I called out for Nell to come in. She peeked her head in first and I waved her inside. With a slick smile plastered on her face, she tip-toed inside and sat on the edge of the bed. Covering the speaker part of the phone with my hand, I questioned her antics.

"Why you actin' weird?"

"Who you on the phone with?"

"O, why?"

"Bae," Omar called for my attention.

"Yeah, I'm here." I side-eyed Nell who just sat there looking silly.

"What time can I expect you home?"

"Later this evening."

"Okay. Let's do dinner and then I can have that pussy for dessert."

Blushing, I nodded. **"I'd like that very much."**

"I'm sure you will. Daddy been wanting you. I'll see you later, okay?"

"Alright. Love you."

"Love you, too." The call ended and I gave Nell my undivided attention.

"So, how'd you sleep last night?"

"I slept well. Them shots did it for me. Then the two glasses of wine put my ass out. Did KK text you when she got home?" KK had decided that she wanted to sleep up under her man and had left a little after nine last night.

"Yep. Move over so I can lay down." She went to move up on the bed, next to me and I stopped her.

"No!"

"No, what?" She asked with a smirk.

"No, ummm, I'm naked."

"Bitch, I knew I heard yo' nasty ass last night." She hit the bed and fell out in a fit of giggles.

"What?!! No, you didn't." Pulling the cover over my head, I wanted to sink into the satin sheets and disappear.

"Oh, I most definitely heard you, honey. You and Skoob were havin' y'all a timeeeee!" I threw one of the pillows at her, and she got a kick out of my embarrassment. "You got you some prison dick, bitch. Come on, tell me, how was it?" I held onto the sheet as she tugged at it to remove it from my face. After the third tug, I finally let go.

"Ughh, you get on my nerves. Were you at the door listening?"

"You know, I started to, but then I went on to my room. You know there's but so much my freaky ass can take. Just know that I heard you."

"I can't talk about it."

"Oh, yes the fuck you can, and you will. Besides, who the

hell am I gonna tell? You know this has been a safe space since we locked in, and it will forever remain that. I don't give a damn how many inmates you fuck."

"Lately, I've been rethinking why I'm friends with your silly ass."

"No need to think, bookie. Everyone needs a real bitch on their team and fortunately for you, you have the realest. I'ma give you some space to shower, change my sheets, and get yourself together while I go get my Sunny Anderson on in the kitchen, and whip us up some brunch."

"You mean your Martha Stewart."

"No, I mean my Sunny Anderson."

I stared at her, clueless as to who that was.

"Girl, she's the black chef that be on The Food Network."

"Ummm, okay."

"Damn shame." Shaking her head, she got up and walked out of the room.

Pulling the sheets back, I got up to shower like she'd suggested. I hated to have to go into the details of last night. Not because I didn't want to share them with Nell. She knew everything about me. My hot ass just didn't want to relive the moment out loud, knowing I wanted to do it again.

After brunch, me and Nell spent the rest of the day, lounging around her apartment. She made me give a detailed account of my virtual fuck session, twice. Like myself, she couldn't believe how bold Cameron was and how easily persuaded I was to hand him the pussy on a silver platter. When I told her how I had my mouth open, licking and sucking the air she could not hold her amusement. By the time she finished taking in everything I'd told her, her next question was, *when would I be tapping in for my next session?* Still adamant that there would be no next session, no matter how much my body wanted it, I told her the same thing I'd told Cameron; this one time was it.

She called bullshit but dropped the Cameron conversation altogether. It seemed the more I talked about it, the more I got the urge to check the text he'd sent that I'd yet to open. I had to get him out of my system before I made it back home to Omar.

"Welp, I'm gonna head home to my man. We have dinner plans." Moving Nell's legs from where they rested on mine, I stood up.

"Okay, boo. I'm glad you came over. We've both been so caught up with work our girl's nights have been far and few."

"I know and we're gonna work on that. A bitch really love you, bookie." I leaned down and rested all my weight on her.

"Well, what's not to love, babe?" Shaking my head, I laughed and pulled back.

"Come lock up." Grabbing my purse and gym bag, I slid my feet into my gym shoes.

Getting up, she hooked her arm in mine and walked me to

the door. "Hey, remember, now that you done had sex with your prison man, you gotta put it on yo' real man tonight."

"Bye, Janelle." With my back to her, I chucked her the deuces.

Once in my car, I sent Omar a text that I was on my way home. He responded that he loved me and would see me in a few. Smiling, I connected my phone to the Bluetooth, and started the car. I felt good about going home to my man, even after what had happened last night. I mean, was it cheating… yes, but it all depends on how you look at it. Nah, who the hell was I kidding, it was cheating.

As I prepared to pull off, a video call came through from WhatsApp. My first thought was to decline the call, but then I felt like he needed to see my face when I told him to stop calling me. Cameron needed to know I was dead serious.

"Cameron, you…" my words got caught in my throat and my nipples hardened at the sight of dick on my screen.

"I'm bout to buss, Camille. Where you want me to nut at, Mama?" His voice was low as he stroked his dick the same way he'd done last night. **"Camille."**

"Yes." I unconsciously bit my lip.

"Shit, ssss, can you open your mouth for me baby? Please."

"I can't, I'm in my car. People can see me."

"Put your phone between your legs so I can nut on her then." The stuff this man came up with to say out of his mouth was just downright nasty and I loved me a nasty nigga.

Unplugging the phone, I opened my legs and slid the phone right in my seat. **"Am I there?"**

"Uh, huh."

"Good girl. Here it comes, Mama. Ooou, ooou, fuck, I'm painting that pussy." He grunted and I looked on in amazement as the cum oozed out of the head of his dick and dripped down his shaft. **"How was your day?"** He asked casually, with the camera now on his satisfied face, and his eyes closed.

"How was my day?" I repeated. **"Cameron, be forreal. Is this really happening right now?"**

Opening his eyes, he looked down at the camera. **"Is what really happening? Am I asking how your day was?"**

"After you just jacked your dick and still have cum residue on your hands."

"If I clean up, can I ask you about your day then?"

"Look, I'm gonna be very upfront with you, as much as I enjoyed last night and the show you just put on, this I can't do. Not only am I in a relationship but I could get fired for this. Can you please just let me enjoy you in my dreams…please." My case of word vomit was so severe, that I'd slipped up and told this man that I had been lusting after him in my dreams. I knew he wouldn't let that part of my statement go over his head.

"Camille, if you're looking for a response that sounds anything remotely like I'm about to respect your relationship or your position at this prison, don't hold your breath.

I really don't give a fuck about none of that, and neither do you. I fuck with the fact that you're trying to be noble about it, though. This dick wants you and that pussy needs me. I can tell by the way she responded to my voice. This is our little secret. I ain't gon' be the nigga to make you risk it all. I'll keep it discreet when it comes to making you skeet."

"This can end badly."

He licked his lips and smirked. "You talkin' bout ending, we're just getting started, Mama. I'ma let you go so you can do the relationship thing. Have a good night."

"Goodnight, Cameron." My hand hovered over the end button, but I wasn't ready to press it.

"You gon' let me go or take me home witchu?"

"I don't think I'm ready to go home, now."

"Oh, yeah? Well, come spend the night with me."

Giggling, I shook my head. "Boy, get off my phone. And make sure you put that thing away."

"What thing, this?" Flipping the phone so that I could see his semi-hard dick, he made it jump.

"No, nasty, I'm talking about the phone."

"Oh," he brought the phone back to his face, "yeah, I got that."

"Okay, goodnight."

"Night." Ending the call, I pulled out of the parking spot with one thing on my mind; Monday morning.

I DON'T KNOW when I'd officially lost my mind but somewhere on my ride home, my car made a detour, and I ended up in the parking lot of the prison. It may have had something to do with the fact that Omar had canceled our dinner plans due to a work emergency, but the closer I got to my destination, I knew that wasn't the case. It had everything to do with me wanting Cameron. In my subconscious mind, maybe I hoped that I was given a reason to take this thing a step further. Either way, I had an itch that only he could scratch.

Dressed in a pair of leggings, an oversized hoodie, a pair of New Balance sneakers, and a well thought out excuse for my visit, I stepped out of my car. Not only was I running the risk of fucking up my relationship but the gossip that went on behind prison walls was worse than anything that *The Shade Room* reported on the daily. There were no secrets in the chain-gang. That alone scared me more than Omar finding out that I was up to no good, but not enough to stop me from prancing my ass right on inside of the building. I needed to see a man about a horse.

I made sure to put Nell up on game as to my whereabouts and put my phone on DND from there. If I was taking it there, I wanted to enjoy my time without any interruption and worry about the consequences afterward, should there be any. Entering the prison, I was relieved to find someone I was cool with working the front desk. My girl, Diedre was on duty and while she was known to have the scoop on anything and everything that went down in the prison. At the same time, the girl was a vault when it came to the people she liked. I happened to be one of those people.

"Hey, girl. What you doing here so late and on a weekend?" Though it was only a quarter to eight, since becoming a Unit Manager, it was rare that I was at the facility after five and weekends weren't mandatory.

Hugging her, I leaned up against the desk. "Paperwork, chile. Nobody told me that once you became the HBIC, all this damn paperwork came with it."

Laughing, she shrugged. "Better you than me, honey. They picked the right woman for the job."

"Can't argue witchu there. I won't be long, though."

"Well, it's been quiet, so I'm sure you won't have any interruptions. LT Davis and Smith are in the control room." Hearing that Kayla was on duty, further proved that the universe wanted this to happen.

"Okay, cool. Let me go in here and get this done so I can go home and climb back in my bed. Oh, and D, I got your lunch for the next week if you didn't see me tonight."

She covered her eyes and turned her head. "Just call me Ray Charles."

Chuckling, I made my way to the back and directly to the control room. From the door, I could see LT Smith on his phone while Kayla was watching a movie on her iPad. Knocking, they both looked up at me. Smith immediately threw his phone down, while Kayla got up to open the door.

"Hey, everything alright?" I asked, looking at Smith, who tried to appear busy, by reaching over the switchboard.

"Ed, it's cool, we're not in trouble," Kayla assured him.

He looked to me for confirmation to which I nodded. "You good. Looks like y'all locked everybody down early."

"Yeah," Kayla answered. "It got a little rowdy after dinner, and you know I ain't going for tussling with these niggas. So, I gave them the option to lockdown early tonight or lockdown for another week."

"I see they made the right choice."

"Indeed. What you doing here?"

"Paperwork." Her eyes lingered on mine for a few seconds as if she was trying to figure out the truth in my statement. "And I need you to pop Haynes' cell. I've been hearing some-things about him and I wanna do a surprise shakedown."

"Really? We can have Ed do it."

"Nah, I got it. He won't expect me to be the one to conduct the search. I wanna hit him with the element of surprise."

Nodding slowly, she pointed to her head. "That makes sense. Okay, I got you. We'll be here if you need us."

"Okay, thanks. Enjoy your movie." I winked at her, and she giggled, knowing that it was against the rules for them to have such electronics out while on duty.

Heading downstairs, I heard Cameron's door pop and when it opened, he was sitting up on the top bunk, eating a bag of chips. When we locked eyes, he smirked, and I signaled for Kayla to close the door. Taking out my phone, I texted her that her next vacation was approved without review so long as she kept her eyes open and Ed busy. Her winking emoji reply was enough to let me know that she was with the program.

"I came to…"

"Get fucked," he finished my sentence and put a chip in his mouth. "I'm already knowin'. I also know we don't have long, so let's get to the business, Sexy."

My pussy juiced up in anticipation. I knew he was going to be everything from my dreams and then some.

Chapter 6

CAMERON

Hearing my cell door pop, the last face I expected to see was Camille's. Standing before me in a pair of tight ass leggings, I zeroed in on her pussy print. Thinking about her perfect titties underneath the oversized hoodie, my dick bricked up. The door closed and I could see her tense up a little. I didn't move nor did I speak first.

"I came to…"

"Get fucked," I interrupted her. "I'm already knowin'. I also know we don't have long, so let's get to the business, Sexy." Eating the last chip from my bag of Lays, I hopped down off the top bunk, tossed it in the trash, and closed the distance between us. Standing in front of her, I licked the salt off my fingers. "Can I take your clothes off?"

She nodded her approval.

Reaching down, I put my hands up under her hoodie and she sucked in a breath as my hands brushed across her soft skin. There was no shirt underneath the hoodie, revealing another black, lace bra once I pulled it over her head. Throwing it on the top bunk, I used my tongue to trace the outline of her breasts.

"Ooohh," she let out, throwing her head back.

Her soft moaning had precum leaking from the head of my dick. She had me feeling like a horny lil' nigga back in high school. I couldn't let her know that, though. Camille had to see that while she had control out there, I controlled what went on in this cell.

Wrapping one hand around her throat, I slipped the other into the front of her leggings, past her panties. "Open your legs." She compiled, and I could feel the heat as it radiated off her sex. "Tell me what I do to you in your dreams, Mama." Continuing to kiss from her jaw to her neck, I rubbed her clit.

"You kiss me."

Pulling my lips from her neck, I placed them on her mouth. The goosebumps that crept up on my arms made me pause. A nigga ain't never felt no goosebumps, not when I was about to fuck.

Camille put her hand over mine and guided my middle

finger inside of her. "You move your finger like this. Sssss, sometimes you go slow," she pecked my lips, "and because I've been wanting you so bad, sometimes slow doesn't work for me and one finger isn't enough. So, you add another." She kissed me again while moving my fingers so that there were two inside of her. "Shit, yes, just like that."

I sped up my movements and I could hear her wetness speaking on her behalf. With my dick threatening to bust through my pants, I swooped her up in my arms and put her up against the wall. Pulling my fingers out of her wet box, I put them up to my mouth and licked her juices off them. Leaning forward, she put the same two fingers to her lips and sucked them sensually.

"Damn, come do a nigga dick like that."

With a smile, she cocked her head to the side. "Let me down." Slowly setting her back down on her feet, I stepped back and watched as she quickly maneuvered out of her shoes and leggings making sure to slide her shoes back on. "We don't have a lot of time."

In the middle of my six-by-eight cell, she squatted in front of me and pulled my pants down to my ankles. My dick was so hard, the veins were poking out that muhfucka. Her eyes lit up and she opened her pretty mouth wide and wrapped it around my shaft. The feeling of her warm mouth and spit as she bobbed her head up and down almost made me scream out like a bitch. It had been four long years and while I'd mastered the art of jacking, it didn't compare to a wet mouth.

"Shit, yeah, oooh you a nasty ass bitch. Eat that dick up, Mama, yesss."

Using her mouth as a suction cup, she sucked me up and jerked my dick at the same time. Between her intense stare, her sexy ass moans, and the spit that slid down the sides of her mouth, I knew it was gonna be over for me at any minute and the alpha male in me just couldn't let her make me buss first.

Gawk, gawk, gawk, gawk. The sounds of her doing my dick the nasty way echoed throughout the small cell. Shorty was in the zone.

"Arghhh, fuck. Mmhmm. I need to feel your walls, Camille. You want me to fill that pussy up?" Still focused on the task at hand, she nodded, not breaking her rhythm. "Come on, let me feel that pussy." Pausing, she released me slowly with a sneaky grin. "Get yo sexy ass over there and bend over."

Taking a couple steps forward, she stopped, and turned back to me. "Can I kiss you again?"

Smiling sheepishly, I cupped her cheeks with my hands and parted her lips with my tongue. As we kissed passionately, she jerked my dick, and there were the goosebumps again. Giving her one last peck, I ordered her to turn around. Stepping out of my pants and boxers, I stroked my dick, while she assumed the position, using the steel rail on the bed for leverage.

"Goddamn, this muhfucka shaped like a heart. Must be a

lotta love back here." Smacking her cheeks, they rippled, and she made her ass clap.

"You betta make me breaking the rules worth it."

"I promise, Mama." Placing all nine inches at her opening, I could already feel the pussy leaking. *God please don't let me get this woman pregnant before I can fully make her mine,* I silently prayed while sliding into her waterpark.

"Ughhh, yesssss, Cameron," she cooed, throwing her ass back. She needed this just as bad as I wanted it. "Please, please stay right there baby. Ooouu, you hittin' something."

"That's yo A spot, Mama. You feel that pussy getting wetter and wetter? Let it go, Baby. Cream all over this dick." Holding onto her thick hips, I hit the same spot mercilessly. She was taking the dick like a champ. Lifting her leg so that it was in the crook of my arm, I reached around and rubbed her clit.

"Ohhh, God, I'ma bout to cum."

"Let that shit go. You betta wet this dick up, too." Swiping up and down her clit, I felt it swell under my touch.

"Oooouuu," her voice trembled, and her body withered as she drenched my hand.

"Good girl, baby." I continued to thrust upward, knowing I was about to be right behind her. "Shitttt!" Dropping her leg, I pulled out of her quickly to avoid busting in her. When her nasty ass dropped down to her knees with her mouth open and tongue out in time to catch the nut, I felt like I'd died and gone to heaven. I came so hard my ears rang. "Ahhhhhhh."

Looking down at her through lazy eyes, I watched her swallow before standing to her feet. "Better than anything I could've ever dreamed of."

Pulling her to me, I kissed her lips. "I hope you know what you just signed up for. I'm on yo' head now."

THE NEXT MORNING, I woke up to my vibrating phone. I'd been sleeping so well, that it didn't dawn on me that I'd left the phone out overnight. Camille had a nigga in a sex coma that I had to shake quickly. Having a phone was a lifeline in prison and I couldn't function at full capacity without one, so I couldn't afford a slip-up. The vibrating stopped before I could answer the call. Checking my notifications, I noticed the missed call from my mother. Tapping the screen to call her back, the phone rang three times before she answered.

"Hey, son."

"Hey, ma. How you feeling?"

She let out a wet cough and cleared her throat before responding. **"I'm fine. You the one acting like I'm on my way outta here."**

"No, I ain't."

"Boy, you called me every hour on the hour, for three hours straight the other day."

"So, you my mama, and you're sick. I'm supposed to check on you." She laughed and coughed again. **"You good?"**

"Yep. This is just a part of the Covid, it'll pass soon. My son, the worry wart. How you doing, baby?"

"I'm good, ma. Just counting down the days till I touchdown."

"Me too, son, me too."

"I already know what I want you to cook and who I wanna see."

"Is that your way of telling me that you don't want me to have a welcome home gathering?"

I chuckled at her catching on so quickly. **"That's exactly what I'm saying. Only our family."** My family consisted of me, her, Sarai, and Keion. Everyone else was just an extension. And it wasn't because I didn't fuck with people, but I'd lay down my life for my three. It was my family that kept me in good spirits during this time, so the celebration was more for them for holding it down in my absence.

"Well, alright, party pooper. If that's what you want."

"It is."

"Can I tell you what I want and would love?"

"Sure, ma. You know the world is already yours."

"I want you to find you a good woman. Preferably someone with ambition, that has her own thing going on, loves kids, and can cook."

My mind went to Camille, and I envisioned her in the kitchen, cooking up a meal for me and me putting this dick on her real good to show my appreciation.

"Cameron."

"Hmm?"

"I said I need you to find you a woman."

"I heard you, Ma. I'm gonna work on it. I'm gonna give you a call a little later, okay? I wanna get up and get myself together."

"Okay. I love you, son."

"I love you, too, lady."

I went to hang up and a call came in from Camille.

"Wassup, sexy."

"Hey, I need you to check around to see if I left something last night."

"Okay, you wanna give me a hint as to what this something is?"

"Umm, it's black."

Sitting up straight, I wiped the cold from my eyes and scratched my head. **"That's all you got, its black?"** My eyes scanned the room and landed on something black next to the toilet. Standing, I went to reach down and pick it up. When I realized what it was, I smirked.

"This is so embarrassing. I left my panties, Cameron."

"I got em'." I swiped the seat of the panties across my nose, and her scent was still present.

"Shit, you have to get rid of them. Uhh, flush em' down the toilet."

"And clog the bowl up? Nah, not a good idea. Why you sound like you ducking and hiding?"

"I'm not. I just got home and I'm not tryna talk all loud.'

"Oh, ya man's an nem' must be home." I didn't like that she was just getting in after being with me. It was super early in the morning. Home should've been her final destination after leaving the prison grounds. "Ay, I hope you ain't out there dick hoppin'."

"Dick hoppin? Boy, please." She laughed but wasn't shit funny.

"You heard me. I gotta breeze, though. They just called for us to line up for count. Don't worry bout your panties, I'll put them in my Bible."

"You'll do what? No, Cameron, that's weird. You betta not."

"Shit, you blessed me last night. I think it's an appropriate place. I gotta go." Ending the call, I stashed my phone away. The cell doors popped, and I stepped out to post up.

"Say, Cam," a dude they called Sleepy who occupied the cell next to me spoke. He was a frequent shopper who always had his paper right. Sleepy was one of the few guys I let talk to me outside of a transaction.

Looking over in his direction, I nodded. "Wassup."

"Them folks hit yo' cell last night? I heard yo' shit pop and wanted to know if I needed to be on point."

"You should always be on point," I said, ignoring the first part of his question. There would never be a time where I divulged any of my business to these niggas. They'd fuck around and have me and Camille on front page news.

"True dat and I do that on the daily. I'm just saying, if they pulled up on yo shit in the middle of the night, should I expect a visit at some point, too."

Hearing names called out in the roll call, I paused to listen out for mine. I watched as LT Davis slowly made her way down the tier. Stopping in front of me, she glanced inside my cell before focusing on my face.

"All good, Haynes?" She questioned, staring me down. On the outside looking in, the way she was postured, it looked like she was about to be on bullshit, but I could see the smile in her eyes.

"Everything is everything," I replied. Winking, she kept it moving.

"Man, I'ma have to start hanging witchu, my boy. The bitches flock to your cell."

I looked Sleepy up and down and shook my head. He was an out-of-shape, ashy-looking nigga with starter dreads that needed loving hands for them to even begin the growing process. His face was filled with dark, acne spots that he may have been able to grow out of as a kid, had he stopped picking at it for five minutes out of the day. We were not the same in any way.

"Man, I'm in prison just like you, these women ain't stuntin' me. Stay on yo' pivot, my nigga." Leaving him standing there, I closed my cell door.

Sleepy mentioning my cell being popped let me know he was keeping tabs on a nigga. I had to put Camille on game. It was quiet on the getting nasty in the cell. As the Unit Manager, I was sure she could think of some other places for me to dig her back out. I was with the spontaneous shit.

Chapter 7

CAMILLE

Saturday night's creep session had a bitch in disarray. The way Cameron made my body feel, there was no way I could return home and sleep comfortably next to Omar after. And I damn sure wasn't about to walk up in the house that I shared with my man knowing that underneath my leggings was just my bare ass. I may have had a lot going on, but I wasn't that trifling. I ended up heading back to Nell's house and spending the night there.

When I did return home the next morning, O was gone and by the way the bed was made up, I could tell that he hadn't slept in it. The crazy thing was, I couldn't press the issue if I wanted to. Not after I'd just spent time behind bars, getting my ass tore up. I simply sent a text to let him know that I was back and went about the rest of my day. When he did make it home, it was late. I didn't note the time, but the kiss he planted on my cheek and the smell of YSL Libre perfume were two things I committed to memory.

He took a shower, snuggled up next to me, and was out like a light in seconds. As a woman who'd just been fucked good the night prior, I knew a sexually satisfied man when I saw one. I'd just left one in prison. Omar was fucking around, and he couldn't have picked a better time to do it. Getting up Monday morning, I did my morning routine and was out the door before he woke up. On my drive to work, I called Janelle to let her in on my suspicions.

"You see, the thing that's pissin' me off is the nigga got the nerve to be out cheatin' but laying mediocre pipe. It's the audacity fa me."

"Nell, I ain't even mad."

"Shit, I know you ain't mad. You let inmate #69 dick you down and now you all zen and shit. I love that for you."

"Not inmate #69," I cackled.

"Clever, huh?"

"Very. But on a serious note, I kinda had a feeling that he may have been fucking around, but I am no longer in

the business of calling a nigga out on they shit when it doesn't directly affect me. Maybe if the dick was hittin' on something I would be mad, but bitch I feel liberated. At this point, since I don't know how long he's been doing his shit nor do I have hardcore evidence, I'ma just move accordingly."

"Meaning…locking in a few dick appointments wit ya boy."

"For as long as he's at the prison, yes."

"You know what I would do?"

"I know whatever it is, it's gonna be some off-the-wall shit."

"Girl, I'd play that shit like one of them hood books. O's ass would be out and big dick Cam would be in. Don't just fuck him, get to know him, and make him yo man when he comes home."

"Ummm, let's be clear, I'm only here for a good time, not a long time."

"Alright. I already see how this gon' play out."

"Well, stay tuned, my girl. I'll call you later."

"Okay. Hey, don't go in that prison skipping and shit. Keep that shit playa how I taught you. You can't let that nigga know the dick is like that just yet."

"Love ya, bye." Ending the call, I walked inside the prison. After a little small talk with Deidre who was at the front desk again, I made my way to the back.

Entering my unit, it was in full swing. The guys were out

and about and there were two officers on the floor, monitoring movement. Feeling eyes on me, I glanced over at Cameron's cell. There he stood, leaning up against the doorway. We locked eyes briefly as I continued towards my office, making sure not to linger. Closing the door behind me, I set my purse down and hung up my jacket. Turning the volume off on my phone, I turned my computer on. While waiting for it to power up, I heard a knock at the door. Getting up, I opened it to find Kayla and Cameron standing side by side.

"Hey, girl."

"Hey," I spoke to her, avoiding Cameron's eyes. "Everything good?"

"Yep. He said he had an issue with his visitor list.

"Oh, okay. Thanks, Lieutenant Davis. I'll take it from here. You can have a seat, Haynes." Stepping back to allow him entry, I told Kayla to stay close by.

"I'll keep an eye out," she assured me. I didn't respond verbally but a nod confirmed my thanks.

Closing the door, I turned to address Cameron. "Do you really have an issue with your visitor's list?"

"Yeah. What, you think I made some shit up just to get in here?"

I wanted to say that was exactly what I was thinking but held my tongue. "What's the problem?" I went to walk past him, and he put his hand on my leg to stop me.

"How'd you sleep last night?"

"How'd I sleep?" I repeated, doing my best to stay focused.

"Yeah. Did I cross your mind?"

I heard Nell's voice, reminding me to keep shit playa, but I was failing the home team. As his hand crept up my leg, my pussy reacted.

"Yes, Cameron," I answered, honestly, "you crossed my mind." Pulling me by my leg so that I was standing directly in front of him, he ran his hand up my thigh, stopping between my legs. "Cameron," I whispered his name, biting my lip as he rubbed my pussy through my pants. My eyes closed, as the friction alone made my pussy wet.

"Come sit on it." Opening my eyes, I looked down and he had his dick out, stroking it. This nigga was like a fucking magician, the way he was able to maneuver without me noticing.

"We can't."

"We can. Didn't you tell me this was your unit when I first got here?"

"And it is, but…"

"No buts. Come sit on it for me, Mama. Please." It was something about the way he said please, coupled with his sexy stare that had me taking one leg out of my dress pants and placing myself on top of him. He swiped his dick up and down my slit, playing in my wetness. "My own little Hurricane Harbor."

Knowing time wasn't on our side and needing a release, I

impatiently guided him inside of me. "Ahhhhhhh," I let out a sound of sheer ecstasy. Leaning forward, I put my lips to his neck and sucked on it while bouncing up and down at a medium pace. I had to keep my face buried in his neck to keep from screaming out. "Mmmhmm, mmmm, mmmm." Grabbing my ass, he spread my cheeks and put his thumb at my asshole. "Oooouu, you gon' make me cum all over this dick."

"You gon cum, Mama? Fuckkk, make me cum witchu. Uh-huh, get all that dick. You like it when I play witcha asshole, huh. Gimmie a kiss, nasty girl. Gimmie a kiss and tell me you love the way this dick feels."

Kissing him hungrily, I bounced faster, feeling myself reaching my peak. "I love the way this dick feels. Oooh, fuck, I'm cummin'." Putting my face back down, I sunk my teeth in his neck.

"Shitttttt, Camille." He held my waist tightly and I could feel his body jerk under me as he filled me up with his seeds. "Damn, I'm sorry."

Breathing heavily, I picked my head up and kissed his lips. "It's okay…I'll take care of it." I didn't know what I meant by that, and he didn't press the issue. Giving him one last peck, I climbed off of him. Redressing, he tucked his dick away and I sat down at my desk. "So, your visitor's list."

"Yeah. I need you to remove Destiny Moore. I requested it a few months ago, and I don't know what wires got crossed, but she was able to make it through. I'd like to make sure that doesn't happen again."

"Destiny Moore. Got it. Will that be all?

"Damn, a nigga come in here and stroke you good and now you kicking me out?"

"Yes, I am. You've been in here long enough already."

"Aight," he stood, "I'ma go. Same time tomorrow?"

Giggling, I shook my head. "Good day, Haynes."

"Keep it tight and wet for me, Mama." Winking, he opened the door and walked out.

Leaning back in my chair, I silently prayed that things would continue to go my way without any hiccups. Hiccups led to exposure, and I wanted to stay deep in this secret for as long as I could...so at the very least, he could stay deep inside me.

I LEFT work feeling good and suddenly had the urge to whip up a meal. Stopping at Whole Foods, I picked up two NY strip steaks, a bag of shrimp, potatoes, and ingredients for a salad. I hadn't cooked a full meal in about two weeks. I wasn't a heavy eater and with O's crazy hours, I didn't see the reason to cook as much. Today, I had an appetite, and steak, sauteed shrimp, garlic mash, and a side salad were on tonight's menu. Hopping back in my car, I put my home playlist on and got ready for the drive. Two songs in, my phone rang with an incoming call from O. Turning the music down, I answered.

"Hey, love."

"Hey, baby. You on your way home?"

"Yes. I stopped at the Supermarket to pick up a few things. You home?"

"Yeah, got in earlier. I wanna take you out tonight to make up for canceling on you at the last minute."

"I have a better idea. How bout we stay in, and I cook? I had a long day, and I don't feel like getting dressed up for dinner."

"Oh, ummm, yeah, we can do that."

"Okay, see you in a few. Love you."

"Love you, too."

The words that we spoke fluently up until two nights ago now seemed strained. Still, I wasn't moved to be sad about it. And it had nothing to do with me not loving Omar because I did. My body had just become separated from my heart. Cameron had my body and Omar…well, he had part of my heart. And it may have always been that way. Knowing who I was at the core of me, there's no way I could've allowed a nigga to even sniff the pussy if my mind, body, and soul were immersed in another man.

I arrived home, to find him in the kitchen, unloading the dishwasher.

"Hey, baby," he greeted, walking over to take the two grocery bags from me. Kissing my cheek, he set them down on the counter.

"Hey, were you cleaning?"

"Just straightening up. I know you don't like dishes to sit in the dishwasher for too long."

"Well, okay, don't let me stop you. I'm gonna get started on dinner."

Washing my hands, I took out the seasonings for the steaks and set them down on the counter. The silence in the kitchen made the flashbacks to sex with Cameron replay loudly in my head. To drown them out, I grabbed my phone and went to my cooking playlist. As I went to hit the shuffle, I got a call from KK.

"Hey, boo, wassup."

"Hey, are you at work?" She questioned and I could pick up on the urgency in her tone.

"No. Why, what's wrong?" My mind went to Cameron.

"Keion just got a call from the prison saying Cam was stabbed. They said he was in the infirmary and now we've been—." My phone beeped, indicating another call. Pulling the phone from my ear, I saw that it was Kayla calling.

"Hold on, KK. I got another call, don't hang up." Clicking over, I didn't give Kayla a chance to speak before asking what happened. I couldn't hide my concern if I wanted to.

"It's bad, but he's going to be okay. He was stabbed in his side, and I was able to see him off to the infirmary." By the way she was whispering I could tell that she was being mindful of what she said and her surroundings. **"I'm gonna call from the tower phone, that way it's on record that I**

reported the incident to you, and you have a reason to come in, okay."

"Okay, thank you so much, Kayla. Whatever you need in exchange for this, its done."

"No need. I've been here before. Got a five-year-old to show for it. Look out for my call." She ended the call after dropping a bomb on me that left me stuck for a second.

"Everything okay?" Omar inquired, with a questionable look on his face.

"Ummm, no. I gotta head back to work. I'm not sure when I'll be back. Sorry about dinner. Just put the steaks in the fridge." Snatching up my purse, I clicked back over to KK. "Hey, I'm headed back that way now." I waited until I was out the door to tell her what Kayla had told me.

"Shit, okay. Bae, Camille is on her way to the prison to check on him." I heard her say to Keion. "Cam, you're on speakerphone."

"Hey, Keion."

"Wassup, Camille. Preciate you doing this. I need you to make sure that my brother is good. And not just good enough by the prison system's standards. I need you to make sure he's straight. I know people and believe me when I say, they don't want me to start making calls. I'll make that bitch a slaughterhouse behind my blood; on some front-page news type shit."

I swallowed hard, taking in his threat. "I'll keep you posted."

"Thank you." Ending the call, I got in my car and prepared for the hour and fort-five-minute drive back to the prison.

Kayla had kept her word and called me while I was en route. Instructing her to lock the unit down, I hit the highway, cutting my drive time by twenty minutes. Entering the building, I checked in and went straight to the infirmary. Seeing Officer Dave outside the door, I made sure to keep a straight face.

"What are you doing here?" He questioned.

"I'm sorry, do I answer to you, or do you answer to me?" Silence. "Okay, cool. Now that we have that established, aren't you supposed to be in there with the nurse and the inmate?"

"I was and she asked me to step out."

"Really? I wonder why. Excuse me." I pushed the door open and turned back to him. "You can go back to the unit. I got it from here." He scoffed and shook his head before walking off. Entering the infirmary, I could hear the nurse talking and assumed that Cameron must've been out of it because I didn't hear him responding.

"Maybe you can give me a nod just so I know that you hear me talking to you," Nurse Parrish said to Cameron, who lay on the hospital bed, with his eyes closed and his arm covering his face.

"Parrish, I called out," making my presence known. She turned to me and smiled.

"Ms. D, how are you."

I returned her smile and nodded. "I'm well, how's the patient?" Cameron hadn't said anything, and his face remained covered.

"Stubborn as a bull, this one. He refuses to take any pain medication. I was able to stitch him up pretty good, so I don't believe he needs to be hospitalized. I'll monitor him over the next week or so to make sure the stitches remain intact. Other than that, superman here is all good."

I moved in closer so that I was at his bedside. "You wanna tell me what happened, Haynes?" I questioned.

"Nah," he let out. "Are we done here?" He asked, finally revealing his eyes. I didn't like the fire behind them.

"Yes, we are," Parrish confirmed. "Oh, and Ms. D, you may wanna do something about that Officer Dave. He's just as mean as I don't know what. I had to tell him to step out and let me do my job."

"I'll take care of it."

Cameron sat up carefully and stood to his feet. I wanted to reach out and help him, but knowing how inappropriate it would look, I just walked alongside him.

"No showers until I give you the okay, Haynes. Those stitches can't get wet."

He nodded his response and took slow steps towards the door. I escorted him back to the unit and into his cell in silence. Making sure he was situated in his bunk, I went to step out and ran into Kayla as I went to close his cell.

"Hey, is he good?"

"Yeah. What the hell happened?"

"Girl, I don't even know. Ain't nobody talking. And the shit happened so fast, the officers that were on the floor missed it. I was out on lunch."

"Anybody run the cameras?"

"It happened behind the steps. Nobody knew he was stabbed until he walked over to the desk and requested to go to the infirmary. But look, you have an hour before Dave comes back from lunch. Do what you will with that information. When it's close to that hour being up, I'll start my final walk around before the end of my shift."

"Okay." I turned to go back in the cell, closing the door behind me.

Against my better judgment, I kicked off my sneakers and climbed into the bottom bunk with him. Intertwining my legs with his, I turned his face towards me and kissed his lips.

"How long we got?"

"An hour. Can you tell me what happened so I can take care of it?"

"No. I don't wanna talk about prison shit with you."

"Cameron, I—."

"Come ride my face. I can't fuck you like I want to cause my side is hurting like a bitch." He winced as he shifted his body.

"That's why you should've taken the pain medication."

"Come ride my face," he repeated. "If that doesn't take

away the pain, then I'll go back to the infirmary and get the medication tomorrow."

"I can't get on top of you in this little ass, makeshift bed. I'd hurt myself. I got you, though." Reaching down, I slipped my hand into his boxers and pulled out his dick. It stiffened at my touch. Kissing his neck, I stroked it. If I could momentarily take the pain away, I was at his service. Stroking and twisting his dick, I deepened the kiss. The seat of my panties was drenched as he ran his tongue over my lips.

"Shit, I'm bout to buss, Mama." Pulling back, I dropped down and replaced my hand with my mouth just as he nutted. I could hear him grunting, as I slurped up everything he had to give, making sure to swallow. Casually putting his dick back in his pants, I laid back. "I'll beat yo ass if you even think about going home and doing to that nigga what you just did to me."

"You can't say that, Cameron."

"The hell I can't. Try me if you want to. I already know how your throat feels, so I'll know if someone else was in there."

"That doesn't even make se—."

"Try me." I went to sit up and he pulled me back down. "What I'm about to tell you is going to sound wild, but I need you to listen and take heed. And as you're listening understand that this ain't no jail talk." His eyes bore into mine as he spoke. "I'm not the type of nigga to step on the next man's toes but I am the type of nigga to go after what I want. I've watched you, studied you in and out of this prison for the last six months. And not on no stalker shit, but because I am intrigued by you. Yeah, the last three days have consisted of fucking and getting off, but I know I ain't been on yo' head for nothing. I have 56 days and a wake-up left before I'm back on the streets. That's how long you have to get yo affairs in order. Close yo eyes, we have 47 minutes before you gotta go." Kissing my lips, he closed his eyes, indicating the completion of the one-sided conversation.

MY RIDE back home was a blur. Silence filled the car as I replayed Cameron's proposal/demand in my head. I think the craziest part of this whole thing was the fact that I was considering everything he said. I thought about the dreams I'd been having, coupled with the way I'd been putting both my relationship and job on the line over the last three days just to be in his presence. I wasn't this careless person by nature, but my actions had shown otherwise. This was supposed to be good fun. It was something to look forward to and he'd made it complicated.

I wanted to call Nell and dump all of this on her, but I already knew what her answer would be. Shit, deep down, I knew what my answer would be but admitting it out loud just sounded wrong. Pushing those thoughts to the back of my mind, I entered my apartment after driving around for hours and headed straight to the bathroom to brush my teeth. As I went to pass my room door which was slightly ajar, I had to do a double take. Surely, my eyes were deceiving me, and I didn't see Omar fast asleep with someone laying on his chest in my fucking bed. Opening the door, I used the flashlight on my phone to get a better look and saw red.

"You son of a bitch!" I screamed out. "Get the fuck up!"

"Oh shit," Omar popped up, just in time to dodge my phone as I threw it at his head. The female was quicker than him, jumping up out of the bed.

"You got me fucked up!" Without thinking, I charged Omar and began throwing fists.

"Wait, hold on," I heard the other voice say. I paused because while the voice sounded feminine, there was a masculine undertone that I could make out.

I went to get off Omar, but he pulled me back down. "Hold on, Camille, just wa—."

"Nigga, let me the fuck go!" I cocked back and hit him in the eye, making him loosen the grip he had on my waist.

"Arghh, shit, Camille!" He yelled out in pain.

Getting out of the bed, I turned on the lamp and gasped at the man that stood before me in a lace front wig, a bra and his hand covering his dick. "You fucking niggas, you greasy bitch?! That's why you can't keep up with me?! Aight, both of y'all wait right here."

Sensing what was about to go down, the he/she snatched up their stuff from the floor and got outta dodge while O tried to move just as fast. Rushing into my closet, I punched in the code to my safe and pulled out my registered 9mm Baretta. Taking it off safety, I marched back into the room and pointed it at O.

With his hands up and his dick out, he tried to reason with me. "Camille, please, let's just talk."

"You fucking niggas?"

"Porsha is transgender."

"Why pursue me if you like men, Omar? Why put my life in danger?"

"We've never slept together without a condom, I swear."

"Nigga, I said, why the fuck would you pursue me if you knew you liked taking dick!" I held the gun steady, ready to do away with his bitch ass for being so careless with my life.

"I…I love you. I was trying to figure things out." As I put my hand on the trigger, my whole life flashed before my eyes, thinking about what I'd be throwing away if I did pull the trigger. Omar wasn't worth all of that. Still, I kept the gun aimed at him.

"Get your shit and get the fuck out of my apartment. And when I say your shit, I mean the clothes you had on. Everything else will be put in trash bags for you to collect when I reach out to you. DO NOT FUCKING CONTACT ME, OMAR!"

"Camille…I—"

"I SAID GET THE FUCK OUT!" Snatching his clothes up from the floor, he ran out the same way his boyfriend had, and I was right behind him. When he stopped to dress himself in the living room, I shut that down. "Nah, nigga, take that shit in the hallway." With his head down, he opened the door and walked out. I slammed it behind him, making sure to lock it.

If this was my karma, God could stick a fork in me because I was too done.

Chapter 8

CAMERON

It had been a month since I was stabbed, and I hadn't seen or spoken to Camille since then. She hadn't posted on IG and when I asked KK about her, all I got was, she was alright. What the fuck was I supposed to do with that? Shit was bothering a nigga to no end, and it wasn't even like me to be hung up about no chick. I'd texted her twice to see if she was okay and the messages hadn't even been read. Figuring that she'd decided that she didn't want to fuck with me on that level, I tucked my wounded pride and focused on my release.

After laying low and plotting, I'd finally caught up with

the nigga who'd stabbed me on some sneak shit. Come to find out, the culprit was the same dude who'd come to shop with me, using Omega's name. Word in the dorm was that the nigga had some built-up animosity about my no credit policy and had it out for me. It just went to show how it was every man for himself behind the wall because I was none the wiser. That junkie ass nigga caught me slipping on the one day I decided to leave my cell for chow.

I ended up finding out it was him just by talks of him bragging about what he'd done. I paid a junkie a sack of cream to air that nigga out, resulting in us being on lockdown for a whole month due to the back-to-back incidents. I was cool with it, so long as I got my revenge. Today was the first day they let us out and it was also visiting day.

"You ready, Haynes?" LT Davis asked, standing at my cell door.

"Yep." I stepped out and she patted me down, before escorting me to the visiting floor.

"Ay, is she okay?"

"I'm sure she is," she replied, without any further explanation.

Annoyed, I didn't press further. Entering the visiting room, I walked over to my brother where he sat with Sarai and KK. With my release date around the corner, I wanted to give my mother a break. Keion volunteered to continue bringing Sarai until that time came.

"Wassup, pretty girl."

"Daddyyy!" She jumped down from KK's lap and over to me. Her excitement never changed. "Daddy, Uncle Keion said you an ugly nigga and he look looks better than you."

KK busted out laughing and Keion smirked. "There you go lyin' on me, big head," he spoke up. "What I said was, he's an ugly ass nigga and I look better than him. Waddup, bro." He stood and dapped me up, giving me a manly hug.

"And we know neither statement is true. Pretty girl, you are the prettiest, and Daddy is the most handsome man in the world. Don't let nobody tell you anything different. What's going on, KK?"

"Everything's good."

Sitting down with Sarai, I listened to her catch me up on all the things happening in kindergarten. She told me about a little scuffle she had over show and tell and I had to stop myself from giving her bad advice on how she could've handled the situation. I didn't play about people fucking with my baby. Kid, adult, animal, anyone could get it when it came to Sarai Amore Haynes. After she was done talking my ears off, she went to get games for us to play.

"Y'all ready for one of those?" I asked Keion and KK.

"Yep. It won't be too long either," Keion answered and looked over at KK, who had a big grin on her face.

"Oh, word?"

"In seven months, you'll be able to wear that uncle title just as proud as me." He rubbed KK's belly and I stood to hug him.

"Congratulations, nigga. Ahh, man, that's wassup. You stuck now, KK."

"Damn, sure is, just like Cami—." She nudged Keion, making him stop talking. I caught the gesture but with Sarai running back over, I couldn't inquire further.

When the visit was over, Sarai was good and tired, falling asleep in my lap. Kissing her forehead, I handed her over to Keion. Saying my goodbyes to the duo, I spoke directly to KK.

"When you see Camille, let her know she has 27 days. She'll know exactly what I'm talking about. Y'all drive safe." She nodded, and they got up and left the visiting room. Whatever Camille had going on, I hoped that she was good and ready for a nigga to pop up.

BACK IN MY CELL, I was ready to lie down and take a nap. Lately, I'd been doing a lot of sleeping and it didn't dawn on me till now how odd that was. I was used to being up from five in the morning when they did first count and staying up a little past midnight. Now, it was nothing for me to be lying down on my phone one minute and the next I was knocked out. I went to close my eyes when my phone vibrated next to me. I didn't recognize the number, so I sent the call to voicemail. When it called right back, I answered after letting it ring a few times.

"Yo?"

"Hey." Hearing Camille's voice, my heart rate quickened for a second. I didn't know what kind of sucker shit I was on, but that shit was making me feel out of place. "Hello, you there?"

"Man, where the hell you been at?"

"I had to take some time off to get my mind right. Had some personal stuff I needed to tend to." She didn't sound like her normal jovial self.

"Talk to me. What happened?"

Sighing, she replied, "It's something I'd rather not discuss. I had some hard decisions to make, and I'm still going through my process."

"Respect." I yawned.

"You sound tired. I'll let you go so you can get some rest. I just wanted to give you a call so that you know that I'm alive." She forced a giggle.

"Yeah, I'm about to take a nap, but I don't want you to hang up. You might fuck around and disappear on me again."

"Shut up."

"I'm deadass serious."

"I'm not gonna disappear, but I wanna take a nap myself, so just text me when you get up."

"We can nap together. Put the phone in the bed with you. Yeah, I know it sounds weird, but if you can give me that pussy on the phone, we can sleep together, too. Come on."

"Do you know what a filter is?"

"Yep. I just don't have one. Now, come lay yo' head on Dada's chest. Whatever it is you got going on, we can talk about it whenever you're ready."

"Okay."

It felt good to hear her voice and I was glad that I let her come to me. Having not heard from her all this time further confirmed that I didn't want to just fuck with her. I wanted Camille to be mine. However, at this point, I didn't know what to expect, so for now I would settle for her being here until I was out there.

CAMILLE

"I don't think this is a good idea." I looked around the diner I sat in with Nell, nervously, shifting in my seat. "I gotta pee." I went to stand, and she placed her hand on top of mine.

"Girl, sit down. You just came back from the bathroom. Everything is gonna be fine."

"How do you know that?"

"Cause I know these things. You gotta relax."

How could I relax when it was the first time, I was going to see Cameron outside of a prison cell? Today was his release day and though we'd been talking every other day since my hiatus, I had created an unspoken distance. Not because I wanted to but because I needed to. I'd even taken a leave of absence from work that was approved with no issue. Omar's cheating had thrown me for an unexpected loop, causing me to have to do a complete 180. The day after I put him and his lover out, I was right in my GYN's office for an emergency appointment to run every STD test they had as well as an HIV test.

I prayed that I didn't come back positive for anything because I knew for sure that I'd be on the bus, being shipped off to a high max security prison for killing Omar's dirty ass. It took two days for me to get my results back and to say I was on pins and needles was an understatement. Now usually, I'd be able to check my online chart to get the results but this time, my doctor called me. As she read off each test and its result, I was sweating bullets. Relief filled my body when everything came back negative.

What I didn't expect was a positive pregnancy test. Yes, positive. And I couldn't dispute the results because she'd taken blood and that was as accurate as it got. After letting that news sink in, I calculated my last period and the last time I'd had sex and by my calculations, me and Cameron had made a love child. The follow-up appointment I had to start my prenatal care confirmed that. It was crazy how it took for this chain of events for me to realize that Omar and I hadn't had much sex in the last few months. I'd been so wrapped up in being satisfied in my dreams, that it hadn't crossed my mind. Now, I was sitting at this diner waiting to drop the bomb on Cameron.

"He is going to lose his mind when I tell him. May not even want anything to do with me or the baby."

"Girl, please, not the same nigga that done had you sleeping on the phone every other night like y'all together. That can't be the same nigga that you think bout to run off and leave you with a kid. And you did what he told you to do, shit, that nigga gon' be ready to decorate a baby room."

"What you mean did what he told me to do?"

"That man told you that you had until he came home to get your affairs in order. You single, right?"

"Right."

"You got all that hoe ass nigga shit out yo place, right."

"Right."

"Affairs sound in order to me." She shrugged and checked her phone. "Oooh, they pulling into the parking lot. And you look beautiful, preggo." She winked at me, and I felt myself get emotional. She knew me like the back of her hand.

For the last month in a half, I'd been complaining about how ugly I felt and how much weight I was going to gain because all I did was stuff my face and sleep. Nell reminded me every day that I was still a bad, beautiful bitch, and my pussy was gonna be even better now that I was pregnant.

Fixing my blazer, I pulled my braids back from my face. KK and Keion walked in first with Cameron bringing up the rear with a little girl in his arms. He was dressed in a pair of grey sweats, and a matching hoodie. It seemed like the standard coming home fit, but the swag he possessed made it sexy. Nell waved the group over.

"Hey, y'all," KK and her round belly greeted us.

"Heyyy," Nell sang, hugging her and giving Keion a half hug.

I stood up to do the same and Cameron remained standing as everyone took a seat. I couldn't read his facial expression and I didn't know whether to speak or not. Passing his daughter off to his brother, he held his hand out for me.

"Come talk to me outside."

I stood and went to walk out with him.

"Here, take your jacket," Nell offered.

"I'm okay." I was already sweating under the blazer due to my nervousness.

"How far along are you?" My mouth dropped open, wondering how he knew. "Close yo mouth. My brother told me, but that's something I should've heard from you."

I dropped my head, knowing I had no argument. "I didn't know how to tell you. And I had a lot going on."

"You sure it's mine?"

"Yes, that's been confirmed by how far along I am. Look, I understand—."

"I didn't think me telling you to get your affairs in order would include finding out you were pregnant with my seed. If this ain't a welcome home present, I don't know what is." He finally cracked a smile. "You can hug me now."

"I don't know if I want to." I grinned and stepped back.

He pulled me back to him and crashed his lips into mine, kissing me like he'd been awaiting this moment.

"I love that you listen to me," he said, pulling a single braid from my face.

"What, the hair?"

He nodded. "Yeah. I need you to keep that same energy moving forward."

"I can't guarantee that."

He kissed my lips and then my forehead. "Oh, you have a lot to learn about me, Mama."

Smirking, he grabbed my hand, and escorted me back inside the diner. Who knew those wet dreams would predict a reality such as this? The Unit Manager and her convict. That shit sounded like something straight out of one of those hood novels that Nell read. Maybe I'd write one of my own one day.

THE END

Did you enjoy the read?

Let us know how much by leaving us a review on Amazon and Goodreads.

Keep reading for a preview of…

Thug Me The Right Way

By DiamondATL & Nai

CHAPTER 1

Kaia

"Girl, get up before you're late for school!" I heard my mother yell from the hallway as she passed through, getting ready for work, I'm sure. Throwing my pillow over my head, I screamed into it. *I just need five more minutes, just five, Lord. Talk to ya girl.* "Kaia Monique Phillips, get yo' ass up before I have to physically remove you from that bed!"

"Okay, Ma. Dang, always tryna get violent." The last part of my statement I made sure to say under my breath. Diane Phillips was nothing to play with. She didn't care that I thought I was grown because I'd just turned eighteen last weekend, she didn't take no shit. Today was my official last day of high school before I graduated next week. Thank God for small favors.

Words couldn't describe how happy I was to leave high school behind. And I had a vast vocabulary, so that said a lot. I was over the teachers, students, janitors, even the lockers. You name it, I was over it. I had dreamed of this day the moment I ended my freshman year. It was time to move on to the next chapter in my life.

Rolling over in my queen-sized bed, I dreaded the thought of having to get out of my twelve hundred thread count sheets and the Tempur-Pedic mattress that lulled me to sleep every night. Sitting up straight, I gave my body a much-needed stretch. Closing my eyes, I thanked God for allowing me to see another day, climbed out of bed, and slipped my feet into my Ugg slippers. Before I could make it to the bathroom, my bedroom door was slightly pushed opened.

"Hey, Stink, you decent?" My sister, Kristen asked through the cracked door with her hand covering her eyes.

"Yes, fool. Come in." I laughed. "I'ma 'bout to hop in the shower." Kristen entered with a big smile on her face and sat down at the desk, next to my bed. "Whatever it is you're about to ask, the answer is no, Bookie." I knew that smile all too well. She either wanted me to sketch something for her to wear or go on a date with her. And let me say, I'd much rather sketch the fit for her and sew.

"Ahh Stink, don't act like that," she dragged out while wrapping her arms around me. "Go take ya shower and I'll tell you wassup once you're out."

"Yeah, uh huh. I'ma let you get it out, but I just feel that my answer is still gonna be no. Mommy leave yet?"

"How you tryna kick me out of my own house?" My mother appeared at my door, fully dressed with her coffee and keys in hand. "Oh, hey stranger, you remembered you had a mama on this beautiful Friday morning?" She playfully chastised Kris before walking in and kissing her cheek. Ever since Kris had moved out a year ago, my mother complained about seeing less and less of her.

"Don't do me like that, Ma. You know I love you. I've just been really busy at the shop lately," Kris said in her defense to which my mom responded with an, "mmhmm."

"I'll be back late tonight, Kaia, so order in. Mase left some money on the table for you. I'll see y'all later, love you." Hugging us both, she left out. My mother was such an inspiration and the epitome of a hard-working woman.

Notice I said, "hard working woman" and not hard-working *black* woman. People kill me wanting to put color on everything. My mother worked as a Charge Nurse at Presbyterian Hospital and had been there for the past ten years. She was such a beautiful woman inside and out. I could never understand how my sperm donor fucked that up.

Kris and I knew exactly who our sperm donor was, he just acted as if he didn't know us. Honestly, it was absolutely fine by me. I considered Mase my dad anyway. Mase was my mom's fiancé. They'd been together for five years and were newly engaged as of six months ago.

He went all out for his proposal, too, making sure to include me and Kristen in ever little detail. He'd been solid since the beginning. Mase gave me and Kris the space to come to him, which helped to build our bond organically. He treated us like queens and for that, he was A1 in my book.

Once my mom left, I made my way to the shower. Being late wasn't an option, even if it was my last day. By the time I was fully dressed in my black slacks and school polo it was seven forty. I had to be out the door by eight to get to school by eight thirty. Happy that Kris was still here, I knew I could catch a ride with her.

"Okay sis, I'm ready, and you have the pleasure of driving me to school."

Looking up from her phone, she smiled. "Oh, the joys of life."

I gave her smart ass the finger. Pulling off my silk scarf, I unwrapped my fresh blow out and let my hair fall nicely pass my shoulders. I had a head full of thick hair that could only be tamed by my stylist and cousin, Heaven.

"Oh yes sister, Heaven did her big one," Kris praised while I brushed my hair, making sure there were no fly aways.

"I know, right. We had a little hiccup at first when she called herself tryna cut it in layers. Ol' scissor happy ass." Giggling, Kris stood up, letting me know she was ready. Applying a coat of Fenty gloss to my lips, I grabbed my MCM book bag, and jean jacket and was ready to go.

"Don't forget your money, Stink," she reminded me, while walking to the door.

Grabbing the hundred-dollar bill from the kitchen counter, I checked its authenticity in the light and nodded.

"Why you checking the money, Kaia?" She laughed, standing at the door.

"Cause, me and Mase been having prank wars for the last week. Last night, I emptied out his whole Casamigos bottle and added water to it." Just thinking about his face when he poured himself a shot had me rolling.

"No, you didn't." Kris cracked up laughing.

"Yes, I did. So, I gotta be careful around here. I can't be walkin' round with no funny money." Slipping the money into my wristlet, I continued on to the door.

"Stuff like that makes me miss home."

"Don't let mommy hear you say that. You'll go back to your apartment and find the U-Haul people witcho shit packed and ready to go."

We both got a good laugh out of the truth in my joke and headed out the door to her new Mercedes AMG truck. I lived comfortably in a brownstone on the Westside of Harlem. With no traffic, my school was a twenty-minute drive. Spring was coming to a close and Summer had crept through, allowing us to ride with the windows down.

"Okay, so what you wanted to talk to me about, Kristen?" I turned a little in my seat to face her.

"Oh, don't hit me with the full first name." She smirked and I did the same. She knew I was on to her ass.

"Okay, so you know Maine, right?"

I looked at her with a raised brow, who didn't know Maine? He was famous on the battle rap scene and known to make moves in the streets. "Yeah, I know of him. Why, wassup?"

"Well, it turns out he's Ant's brother and seeing as though we're going on our first date, I was thinking…"

"Ahh hell naw," I cut her off before she could continue. "Nope, nah, uhn uhn. You always do that, Kristen. You can't go on just one damn date by yourself?" I already knew the answer to my own question; I don't know why I even bothered asking.

"You know the first date has to be a double date to feel him out. If you don't like him, I don't date him." It was that simple for her. We were two peas in a pod. Although she was three years older than me, we had always been on the same level mentally and she valued my opinion.

"You lucky I love you, chick," I said, conceding, without much of a fight. "Where we going?" Low key, I was crushing on Maine. I had never spoken to him, but I'd seen him around a handful of times and baby boy was something special. Standing at six foot one with a low fade, he was the definition of *waves on swim, so they hate on him.* His butterscotch skin tone complimented my bronze glow. I just knew we'd make pretty babies. Finding out he was Ant's brother was quite a surprise.

Ant, short for Antwon, was a big deal in the streets. He had been trying to get close to Kris for a while now. In the beginning of the chase, she was fresh off of a breakup with her ex, Kane. That was one fucker I could not stand. I was still holding onto the hope that he'd go to sleep one day and never wake up. I liked the fact Ant was persistent in the chase. My sister deserved all the happiness in the world.

"Hello, earth to Kaia. Did you hear anything I just said?" She snapped her fingers at me.

"You want me to lie?" I fired back with a smirk, making her mush me.

"You so ignorant yo'. What I said was, we're going to Clyde Fraziers. Ant don't believe we can ball."

"They never do," we said in unison. It was true, nobody believed we knew how to play basketball because of how prissy we appeared to be. It was one of the two things our sperm donor had taught us. How to play ball and that niggas ain't shit, him being the prime example.

"I'll let him know we're on for next Friday night, cool?" I nodded my confirmation. "Good, now get outta my car." We'd pulled up in front of my school quicker than I thought. Loosening my seatbelt, she playfully nudged me to get out.

"Girl please, I've been kicked out of better places." Sticking my tongue out at her, I closed the door.

"Yeah, okay, keep that same energy when you wanna borrow it." Now she was getting carried away.

"Okay, okay sorry and I love you." I quickly back-pedaled, knowing at some point during the summer, I planned on stunting in her car.

"Yeah, I bet. Have a good day, love you, too."

With that, she drove off, leaving me to face the day. *Alright Kaia, this is the last day before graduation, you can do this.* I had to coach myself before stepping into the building. I wondered if my girls, Mecca and Shanice had the same slow start as me this morning. Who am I kidding? We all felt the exact same way about school. We were past the point of ready.

Mecca and Shanice were cousins who couldn't be more different personality wise and in the way they were raised. Mecca liked to be in the mix, and with her mom not being as strict as mine, she was able to rip and run until her heart was content. Shanice, on the other hand, was similar to me. While we were both very social, there were certain things our parents weren't letting us do. Either way, we blended well, and I wouldn't change my crew for the world.

From the freshmen to the seniors, everybody knew us. Each one of us gave main character energy. Some people loved it and others hated from the sideline. And that was a good thing because my attitude was something vicious. One of those sideline haters was Kandice Thompson.

I just knew the mere thought of me, made her mad. It showed anytime we were in the same space. I was a vibe and in a class of my own. I didn't do too much and even still; I posed a threat. Shit, if I was her, I'd probably hate me, too. Putting on a welcoming smile, I got ready to tackle the last day.

"Girl, wake up, class is over," I whispered harshly while shoving Mecca awake. Our AP History class had just ended and she'd slept through most of it.

"Aight, I'm up. This class so goddamn boring. I'm glad it's over and done with." She stretched and straightened out her clothes.

"While you at it, cuz, get that drool on the side of your mouth." Leave it up to Shanice to make a joke.

"Bitch, shut up, acting like yo' ass wasn't sleeping, too." Mecca laughed, balled up a piece of paper, and threw it at Shanice.

"Beauty sleep, baby, beauty sleep," Shanice countered, using her compact mirror to make sure her face was good.

"Beauty sleep my ass, both y'all hoes was knocked out. Come on before we late for Mrs. Battaglia's class." I got up to walk out, and they followed.

"Yes ma'am," they responded in unison. The one class we didn't play about was English. Mrs. B was a beast, but she was my favorite teacher. Her class just so happened to be one of two classes I had with Kandice's crooked letter I shaped ass.

"Alright, ladies and gentlemen, being that this is your last day in my class, I'd like to give out some awards I personally created," Mrs. B announced once we all were seated.

"Y'all sit back and keep it cute cause you know we each have our name on one of those awards," I let both Mecca and Shanice know. They nodded in agreement.

I didn't hang with dummies; my girls were just as smart and talented as me. As Mrs. B called out different names, just as I predicted, my girls collected one each. By the time she'd gotten to the last name, I was on the edge of my seat.

"This last award goes to a student who has surpassed my expectations with her writing skills and dedication to the arts."

"Come on Mrs. B, give my girl her award so she can make these hoes sick," Mecca jumped up from her seat and blurted out.

"Have a seat, Shamecca, and watch your language," Mrs. B scolded.

Holding her hands up, she sat back down. "My bad, my bad, do you." The class snickered and so did Mrs. B. She was used to Mecca's outbursts and antics.

"As I was saying, this student has done her *big one*, as you all say. I'm happy to present this award to Kaia Phillips." Getting up to receive my award, I moved with style and grace as the class clapped and congratulated me.

"Yess, go friend! Y'all better show out for my girl, haters included," Shanice implored while looking in Kandice's direction.

I gave Mrs. B a quick hug and accepted the small plaque. "First, I'd like to thank the Academy…" The class roared in laughter and I giggled before continuing. "Nah, forreal though, thank you Mrs. B for acknowledging my skills and helping me perfect my writing. I also want to thank all of you for being great material as well." Throwing up the peace sign, I sashayed back to my desk.

The rest of class was a breeze and that was appreciated. The bell rang and we were off to the next.

"Aight y'all, three more classes to go and we out this nasty." I was so geeked.

"Yes, I can't wait to cut up this weekend like, *Mecciana, 'bout to graduate high school, graduiana.*" Even though the last part sounded dumb, Shanice and I joined in, doing the buss down dance with her.

"Ayee, buss down graduiana, I wanna see you buss down." We laughed, hyping each other up until I felt myself getting bumped. "What the fuck!" I yelled and turned around. My eyes instantly landed on Kandice and the two pitbulls she hung out with. I didn't refer to them as pitbulls to be funny either. Her friends were really strong in the face. I was convinced that Kandice only hung out with them because she was prettiest out of the trio. "You just couldn't wait until after graduation to get yo' ass whipped, huh? You want your black eye expedited," I threatened, handing my book bag to Mecca.

"Bitch, please. I wouldn't even waste my time. Come on

y'all, ghetto is contagious." Her scary ass walked off once she saw the crowd forming.

"Friend, just let me beat her ass for you," Mecca offered. "Unlike yo' mama, all mine gon' ask when the school call is if I won." She handed me back my bag and I held it in the hook of my arm.

"Right. Aunty Rita be cuttin' up," Shanice cosigned. "Kandice ain't worth yo' time though, friend. She just mad cause her nigga still checking for you. Come on so we can finish out this day."

We moved about the hallways, to our next class without incident. Kandice's beef with me went back to our freshman year, on our second day of school.

I had just walked into the cafeteria, in search of a table for me and the girls to sit at. They'd stayed behind in math class a few extra minutes to discuss the syllabus. Finally finding a table amongst the crowd, I sat down and pulled out my phone to keep me occupied.

"Hey, beautiful, how'd you manage to smuggle yo' phone in here?" I looked up to see who was talking to me and took note of the hazel eyed cutie who stood in front of me. He put me in the mind of Omarion's brother, O'Ryan, only taller with a low-cut fade.

Snickering, I responded. "I didn't smuggle anything in. I walked in with my phone like the gangsta I am." I flexed, making him laugh.

"Oh, aight, gangsta. What's your name?" He asked, taking an unoffered seat.

"So, you bold, huh? You just gon' sit down without asking, okay. My name is Kaia, and you, bugaboo?" I joked.

"Aaron. I see you got jokes, gangsta."

"A lil' something, something." We sat and chopped it up until the girls showed up. They introduced themselves and we continued to talk throughout the lunch period. As we were leaving out, Aaron asked for my number. Before I could shoot him down, his name was called from across the cafeteria.

*"**Aaron!**" The female voice called out with much aggression before walking over with two girls behind her.*

"Looks like you got some company, bugaboo." I was cursing his smooth-talking ass out in my head, but my face remained straight.

The girl grilled me before going in on Aaron who looked uninterested. Not one for drama due to my hands having a mind of their own, I removed myself from the equation. I wasn't for the goofy shit. It just so happened that the same girl was in my fifth period class. This was the one class I didn't have with Shanice and Mecca. As I maneuvered around the seats, I found one to my liking near the window. Pulling out my books, I prepared to get my learn on.

"Listen, I know you're new here and all, but Aaron is off limits, okay?" The girl stood over me, staking claim to her so-called man.

*"We all new here, sis. We're freshmen, remember? Meaning we all just started. And instead of coming to me, let **him** know that **I'm** off limits as well. Now, you're invading my personal space, and it's making me feel threatened. Soon, I'ma feel like I have to protect myself." Pushing back from the table, I let her know in not so many words that I was with the shits.*

"Yeah, aight," was her weak ass response before walking away. I knew a scary bitch when I saw one and Kandice was the scariest.

That's where it all started and still, Aaron had been on my bumper every chance he got. He was well aware that his ass had been friend zoned and it still didn't stop him. We had finally completed our last class and I couldn't be more ecstatic. We were getting our cap and gowns at the graduation, so at this point, we were free to roam the streets.

"Yo', y'all coming to my farewell party tonight?" Aaron pulled up on us as we congregated at my locker. His question was posed to the group, but he stared directly at me.

"Farewell party? Where you going, boy?" I inquired.

"You ain't know? I got accepted to USC, baby," he announced with a Kool-Aid smile on his face.

"Ahh, I forgot they announced that. I didn't think you'd be leaving so soon. Give me a hug, bugaboo, I'm gonna miss your annoying ass." Pulling him in for a hug, my body tingled as he squeezed me tight. Although I hadn't given him any play, I was still very attracted to Aaron. Not only was he fine, but smart as hell and an all-around athlete. I was genuinely happy for him.

"Well damn, how long y'all gon' hug for?" Hearing Shanice, I quickly broke our embrace and he shot me a sly smirk.

"Hater," he joked.

Confirming our attendance, I locked arms with the girls, we walked off. It was time to plan for how we were gonna kill this party. Instead of going straight home, we headed to Mecca's house. Her house was always lit on Fridays due to her mom's weekend card games with her homegirls. We rode the train to Concourse Village, in the Bronx, and walked the two blocks to her house.

"Look, before we go in here, I want y'all to know my mama is trying out a new look." We looked at Mecca confused but let her continue. "Don't y'all *dare* laugh. Matter fact, don't even comment on it, got it?" We both nodded. I had a feeling she was being over the top, so I ignored her. She opened the door and the smell of chicken frying hit my nose, making my stomach growl.

"That you, Mecca?" Her mom called out from the kitchen.

"Yeah, Ma. Kaia and Sha here, too, so I hope you're decent." Ms. Lynn was known to wear some crazy things and would cuss you out if you had something to say about it.

"Girl, please, this my damn house. You lucky I ain't ass naked. Hey, my soon to be graduates." She came out of the kitchen and I legit had no words. Respectfully, I returned the hug she gave me while mouthing, *"what the fuck?"* to Mecca, who just shook her head. Ms. Lynn had platinum blonde finger waves in her head and had topped it off with gold glitter.

As if on cue, Shanice started her aunt up. "Yess, aunty, come through serving the people a blonde moment." She spun her around and Ms. Lynn posed like she was killing the game. It wasn't the style that got me, but the color choice on her midnight complexion had me blown. Once Shanice was done giving her props, we headed to Mecca's room.

"Sha, you know you ain't shit," I said before busting out laughing. Sha held her stomach from laughing so hard.

"Y'all stop clowning my mom," Mecca scolded us, trying not to crack up herself.

"Aight, I'm done, but you need to tell yo' mama that's not the style for her. She walking around here looking like an extra in an Uncle Luke video." I couldn't stop myself from falling out in a fit of giggles again. "Okay, I'm done, I'm done forreal this time." I got myself together and focused on helping her pick out what she would wear to the party. We were celebrating Aaron and most importantly, being a part of the graduating class of 2020.

Available Now On Amazon

ALSO BY AUTHORESS NAI

Thug Me The Right Way

Elevated By His Gangsta Love

Bossin' Up On The Plug

Bossin' Up On The Plug 2

In The Trenches With My Hitta

In The Trenches With My Hitta 2

Stealing A Queenpin's Heart

Stealing A Queenpin's Heart 2

A Piece of A Hustler's Heart

A Piece of A Hustler's Heart 2

A Thug's Love Mended My Heart

A Thug's Love Mended My Heart 2

A Summer To Remember With My New York Bae

A Summer Fling In New York

His Hood Love Gave Me Life

His Hood Love Gave Me Life 2

My Thug, My Sanctuary

Thug Kisses For Christmas

For The Love Of My Savage

Charge It To The Game

Charge It To The Game 2

A Summer To Remember With My Hitta

Snatched Up By A Hitta

Santa Sent Me A Real One For Christmas

OTHER BOOKS BY

<u>URBAN AINT DEAD</u>

Tales 4rm Da Dale

The Hottest Summer Ever

Hittin' Licks For The Holidays: Atlanta

By **Elijah R. Freeman**

Despite The Odds

By **Juhnell Morgan**

Good Girl Gone Rogue

By **Manny Black**

Hittaz

Hittaz 2

Hittaz 3

Hittaz 4

Coldhearted

By **Lou Garden Price, Sr.**

Charge It To The Game

Charge It To The Game 2

A Summer To Remember With My Hitta

Snatched Up By A Hitta

Santa Sent Me A Real One For Christmas

By **Nai**

A Setup For Revenge

By **Ashley Williams**

Ridin' For You

Trickin' on a Heaux for Christmas: A BBW Love Story

Homie Hoppin' For The Holidays

By **Telia Teanna**

The State's Witness

The State's Witness 2

The State's Witness 3

By **Kyiris Ashley**

Stuck In The Trenches

Stuck In The Trenches 2

By **Huff Tha Great**

The Swipe

By **Toōla**

Melted the Heart of a Menace

By P. Wise

Merry Trapmas: Ice & Frost

By **Mia Sky**

Thug Me The Right Way

By **DiamondATL & Nai**

<u>**Coming Soon From**</u>
URBAN AINT DEAD

The Hottest Summer Ever 2
THE G-CODE
How To Publish A Book From Prison
Tales 4rm Da Dale 2
Wet Dreams On Lockdown: The Nurse
By **Elijah R. Freeman**

Hittaz 4
Coldhearted 2
By **Lou Garden Price, Sr.**

The Swipe 2
By **Toola**

Good Girl Gone Rogue 2
By **Manny Black**

Despite The Odds 2
Hittin' Licks For The Holidays: Chicago
By **Juhnell Morgan**

Charge It To The Game 3
By **Nai**

Ridin For You, Too
Wet Dreams On Lockdown: The Female C.O
By **Telia Teanna**

A Setup For Revenge 2
Wet Dreams On Lockdown: The Librarian
By **Ashley Williams**

A Gangsta's Last Kiss
By **Mia Sky**

Pretti & The Beast
Wet Dreams On Lockdown: Lieutenant Grace
By **P. Wise**

Wet Dreams On Lockdown: The Counselor
By **Paris Iman**

Wet Dreams On Lockdown: The Male C.O
By **Tamyra Griffin**

Wet Dreams On Lockdown: The Captain
By **TN Jones**

Wet Dreams On Lockdown: The Warden
By **Shawnice**

BOOKS BY

URBAN AINT DEAD's C.E.O

<u>Elijah R. Freeman</u>

Triggadale

Triggadale 2

Triggadale 3

Tales 4rm Da Dale

The Hottest Summer Ever

Murda Was The Case

Murda Was The Case 2

Murda Was The Case 3

Hittin' Licks For The Holidays: Atlanta

STAY CONNECTED

Follow
Elijah R. Freeman
On Social Media
FB: Elijah R. Freeman
IG: @the_future_of_urban_fiction

www.ingramcontent.com/pod-product-compliance
Lightning Source LLC
Chambersburg PA
CBHW071154300726
48975CB00004B/1150